Did She Want To Interest Rex Jones?

Against her better judgment, against every rational cell in her brain, Lu knew she did. They probably had nothing at all in common; he wasn't even from Culhane County, but from Texas, of all places! Somehow she couldn't see him moving into the rooms behind the Andrew C. Lavender Memorial Gallery.

Tallulah Jones, she mused. Mr. and Mrs. Rex—

Oh, for crying out loud! One date and she was printing up wedding announcements. There were other alternatives. This was hardly the Dark Ages, even if it sometimes felt that way in this town. With a little discretion, a woman could have a perfectly lovely affair with no harm done and no one the wiser.

How would she handle it if he tried to seduce her?

How would she handle it if he *didn't*?

Dear Reader:

Welcome! You hold in your hand a Silhouette Desire—your ticket to a whole new world of reading pleasure.

A Silhouette Desire is a sensuous, contemporary romance about passions, problems and the ultimate power of love. It is about today's woman—intelligent, successful, giving—but it is also the story of a romance between two people who are strong enough to follow their own individual paths, yet strong enough to compromise, as well.

These books are written by, for and about every woman that you are—wife, mother, sister, lover, daughter, career woman. A Silhouette Desire heroine must face the same challenges, achieve the same successes, in her story as you do in your own life.

The Silhouette reader is not afraid to enjoy herself. She knows when to take things seriously and when to indulge in a fantasy world. With six books a month, Silhouette Desire strives to meet her many moods, but each book is always a compelling love story.

Make a commitment to romance—go wild with Silhouette Desire!

Best,

Isabel Swift
Senior Editor & Editorial Coordinator

DIXIE BROWNING
Along Came Jones

Silhouette Desire

Published by Silhouette Books New York

America's Publisher of Contemporary Romance

Books by Dixie Browning

DIXIE BROWNING,

one of Silhouette's most prolific and popular authors, has written over thirty books since *Unreasonable Summer*, a Silhouette Romance, came out in 1980. She has also published books for the Desire and Special Edition lines. She is a charter member of the Romance Writers of America, and her Romance *Renegade Player* won the Golden Medallion in 1983. A charismatic lecturer, Dixie has toured extensively for Silhouette Books, participating in "How To Write A Romance" workshops all over the country.

Dixie's family has made its home along the North Carolina coast for many generations, and it is there that she finds a great deal of inspiration. Along with her writing awards, Dixie has been acclaimed as a watercolor painter, and was the first president of the Watercolor Society of North Carolina. She is also currently president of Browning Artworks, Ltd., a gallery featuring fine regional crafts on Hatteras Island. Although Dixie enjoys her traveling, she is always happy to return to North Carolina, where she and her husband make their home.

One
***

Rex Jones wasn't given to making snap decisions. That was probably why it took him eleven and a half days to fall in love with Mrs. Lavender.

Actually the process began even before he knew she *was* Mrs. Lavender. Certainly before he'd ever heard of Parrish Falls's chief claim to culture, the Andrew C. Lavender Memorial Gallery of Art.

Parrish Falls was one of those small Carolina towns that nestles—as the Chamber of Commerce likes to put it—in the foothills of the Blue Ridge Mountains. But even the chamber turned its back on Parrish Falls in early August, when the heat could flatten a visitor out like a hot sweaty palm.

In the fall the colors could be spectacular, but in August the reddish cast of the dusty sourwoods made a man wonder if someone hadn't snatched a few pages from his calendar while he was busy trying to work in one more short trip to the beach.

Rex Jones wasn't wondering about beach vacations. But then, he hadn't been thinking about the color of the sourwoods that hugged the shoulders of Power Plant Road, either. When he'd spotted the glint of water through the trees, he'd been thinking about a long, cold shower and an equally long, cold beer. At the possibility of spending the next few hours stripped down to his boxers, floating on his back on an icy, spring-fed pond, he touched the brakes, slowing enough for the chalky yellow dust that seemed to hang in the motionless air to settle over the van.

He saw the car first—a dark blue Chevy, well kept, but far from new. It was pulled off the graveled road into the shade of a granddaddy of a white oak tree. And then he saw the woman.

Swearing reverently, he touched the brakes again. It occurred to Rex that he'd seen weeping willows that were less graceful.

He'd seen panhandlers who were better dressed, too.

On the pretext of waiting until she reached her car so as not to cover her in dust, he switched off the engine, rolled down his window and openly watched the woman saunter up the hill toward the road. The tops and tongues of her high-topped green sneakers flapped with every step. She was wearing age-whitened jeans that were worn thin enough to hint at pink thighs, a shirt that was either badly stained or badly faded—he couldn't tell which—and a man's yellow duck-bill cap that sported the logo of a local farm implement dealer.

He studied the hip action necessitated by the steep climb with deep appreciation. What was that phrase he'd read in a sports car ad last week? Poetry in motion? She was that, all right. There were circles of wetness under her arms, and he could see the sheen on her face even from where he sat. He'd be willing to bet it hadn't come from any icy dip, either.

Not until she'd almost reached her car did he even notice what she was carrying, and then a slow grin split his craggy features, fanning crow's-feet at the outer corners of eyes that were inclined to be guarded, and deepening the grooves that scored his tanned cheeks. The lady had been fishing. Possibly even poaching. Over her shoulder she carried a cane pole, and from her hand swung a stringer of bass and bluegills that would easily tip the scales at five or six pounds.

He couldn't resist. "Got a license for those things, lady?" He watched her gaze dart from his face to the door of his van and back again before she replied.

"Live bait and private property. Do I need a license?"

Evidently she'd been relieved to see his JRJ Engineering logo instead of the local fish-and-wildlife insignia. Her smile as she dug into her pocket for her keys could easily have started a core meltdown. "No, ma'am, I don't reckon you do at that. Fine-looking bunch of fish," he said. Fine-looking bunch of woman, too, he thought.

"I'll be giving most of them away."

He tried to think of some compelling remark that would keep her there a little longer. After several awkward moments had passed, he swallowed hard and decided to make a stab at it. "Sure do need some rain," he remarked.

Oh, yeah, that was really fascinating! Disgusted to discover that his once faultless technique had inexplicably deserted him—lack of practice lately, no doubt—Rex cleared his throat and tried again. "Hot for this time of the year, isn't it?"

He winced. It was August, for cripe's sake! What the devil had happened to his brain in the past few minutes? The way he was sounding, someone might think he'd never even *seen* a woman before! Since about age fifteen, he'd had his share of time with the fairer sex—and he liked to think he'd left most of them happier for the experience. Not once did he recollect sounding like such a jackass.

"Even in the mountains, it gets hot in August." Her voice was every bit as nice as the rest of her, he decided. "We're in a valley that seems to trap the heat."

"Oh. Yeah, I guess that's right, isn't it?" She was standing beside the road, and he was still sitting in his van like a damned barnacle, but he was afraid if he made a move to get out, she would leave. "Nice, though. Real pretty country here."

She smiled at that, and he felt a fresh river of sweat trickle down his chest and puddle around his belt buckle. A mouth, two eyes, a nose, a scrap of a chin—what was so special about them? He'd seen that same general assortment on thousands of women and it hadn't affected him this way.

In fact, there wasn't a single thing about her that could be called seductive, yet she was the most alluring woman he'd seen in all his born days. With a stringer of fish, yet!

"Well...I guess I'd better get these things in out of the sun," she said in that soft, husky little voice that only added to the effect she was having on him.

Rex swallowed hard. He was torn between an urge to get the hell out of town while he was still able to function and an even stronger one to proposition her on the spot. He seriously considered offering to dress her catch, cook them for her, cut them into bite-size pieces and place each luscious morsel between her lips with his own fingers.

"Umm...thanks for not powdering me with dust. We really do need that rain, don't we?" Without waiting for a response, she sauntered over to her car, dropped her catch into a plastic ice chest and slid under the wheel.

Slightly dazed, Rex wiped his forehead. The lady could hunker down at his campfire any old time!

Not until after she'd disappeared in her own cloud of dust did it occur to him that he might have taken down her license number. She probably belonged to one of these farms around there.

On the other hand, he didn't particularly care to instigate contact with any branch of law enforcement, not even the DMV. He was now a legitimate businessman, a consulting engineer with the right to add P.E. for professional engineer after the name John Rex Jones on his business cards, but some instincts died hard.

He was also a rambler, had been for years. A drifter, some might call him. But that was only because he was in a position to be able to pick and choose among the jobs he was offered, taking only those well away from his home state, where the name John Rex Jones might trigger a few diehard memories. No law against that.

As a specialist in power plant conversion in a time when such factors as OPEC, Chernobyl and acid rain were constantly shifting the fuel balance, he could work anywhere in the country. It was nobody's business but his own if most of the jobs he accepted happened to be east of the Mississippi.

Rex rolled up the window and switched on the engine, allowing the air conditioner to chill him down again. Briefly he considered getting a cold drink from the cooler in back of the van and strolling down to the pond, but he dismissed the idea as soon as he recognized it for what it was—a futile attempt to prolong an intriguing situation. She was long gone, and besides, he needed a shower.

He needed a break, actually. That was probably the reason he'd overreacted—too much work, not enough play. He was well paid for his efforts, and the truth was, he didn't really need the money. But when all there was was work, what else could a man lose himself in?

It was strictly by choice that JRJ Engineering consisted only of himself and the part-time services of a friend's wife. His office was a separate phone line into Max and Chloe Beal's Richmond home, a room in their attic where he stored files and out-of-season clothing and the use of their address as a mail drop. The arrangement suited him just fine, and with a kid coming and Max still in medical school, the Beals could use the extra money.

Oh, what the hell—maybe he would take a little R and R after he wound up this job. One of these days he was going to wake up and discover that he'd forgotten how to unwind.

It was four days later, on a Sunday morning to be exact, when Rex saw the lady fisherman again. She wasn't fishing this time, she was roasting marshmallows. Over an open fire. In the rain!

Instantly forgetting all his reasons for returning to the job on a Sunday morning, he pulled off the road beside the blue Chevy and climbed out of his van. The grove where she'd taken shelter was about halfway between the road and a crescent-shaped pond that looked to be about eight acres.

"Fish not biting today?" he called by way of greeting.

Lu Lavender glanced up from the marshmallow she'd just incinerated, startled to see a stranger swinging down the hillside toward her. She knew practically everyone in Parrish Falls. Everyone in Culhane County, for that matter. The face looked vaguely familiar, but surely she'd have remembered the rest of him if she'd ever seen him before. He was a rock slide of a man, all hard planes and sharp angles. And *big*! At least six three and a couple of hundred pounds. Not fat, though—just lean, hard muscle attached to a solid frame.

He ducked under the tree, and unconsciously her grip tightened on the sharpened stick she was holding. "Nice string of fish you caught last week," he said, his voice deep, his smile reassuring.

She couldn't quite place the accent. It was Southern, but definitely not local. Yet he looked so familiar....

"The van! You're the same man who stopped last Wednesday so that I wouldn't choke on your dust."

"Correction," Rex said gently, squatting, uninvited on one heel, "I stopped because I was planning on sneaking a swim, and then I saw you and your fish, and I wanted a better look at your, ah, catch. Largemouth and bluegills, wasn't it?"

Lu laughed. "Right. One of the bluegills was enormous—at least a pound. I always split my catch with the man who owns the pond for letting me fish there. Naturally he took that one." There was nothing even faintly alarming in his manner, and he had a wonderful smile—sort of long in coming, but well worth the wait, chipped tooth and all.

Still, it might not be a good idea to encourage him. She'd been warned about the way men preyed on widows by nearly every woman in Parrish Falls after Andrew had died. "Well...looks like the shower's almost over. I suppose I'd better be getting back," she said almost reluctantly.

"Back to fishing?"

"No, Mr.—"

"Jones," he supplied quickly. "Rex Jones."

"No, Mr. Jones, back home. And now, I won't keep you any longer, as you were obviously on your way somewhere else."

It had been a perfectly courteous dismissal, Lu told herself as she watched him rise to his considerable height and nod politely. In a way she was sorry to see him go, but the truth was, he should have known better. She should never have lingered to talk to him the other day, but even so, he should have known better than to try to build on a chance encounter. It should have been obvious to anyone that she wasn't the sort of woman who encouraged that sort of thing. In her position, she couldn't afford to.

He didn't look back. She watched him all the way to the top of the hill, noting the way his khakis embraced his muscular thighs with each long stride, and the pyramid of dampness on the back of his tan shirt that exaggerated the breadth of his shoulders. Surely they couldn't be *that* wide! They only looked that way because his hips were so narrow, his waist so spare.

With a snort of disgust, Lu told herself that the heat was beginning to affect her brain. Picking up the bag of marshmallows, she carefully doused her tiny fire and scattered the coals in the rain-wet grass before retrieving her fishing gear. He'd been right. The fish hadn't been biting. But then, the fish were just an excuse to drive out here each week, to be completely alone for a few hours, to unwind and maybe pretend for a little while that the farm still belonged to her grandparents and that she still slept in the tiny room under the eaves, waking before sunup each morning to do her chores before she climbed behind the wheel of the big orange school bus to begin her route.

*   *   *

Monday. The Tennisson was due to arrive today, and Lu had a thousand things to do first. The art gallery that took up three rooms in her house was strictly a nonprofit affair. Unfortunately. To support that and herself, plus the impractical old house she'd inherited at her husband's death, she worked four and a half days a week—plus too many nights in early April—for Richards and Scott, a local accounting firm. Between her weekday job and her docent duties at the gallery, there was always a bit too much to do and too little time to accomplish it, but then, Lu knew very well she wasn't the world's most efficient worker. Especially when her heart wasn't truly in either of her two jobs.

The whole gallery had to be rehung to make room for the special exhibit. She'd hoped nobody would show up yesterday so that she could get started on it, but a busload of teachers had arrived at three and stayed until almost six. After she'd closed up, she'd made herself a sandwich and munched on it while she started taking down the paintings, her mind straying a little too often to the tall stranger who'd joined her beside the pond earlier in the day.

It had started raining again just after dark, and rain always made her sleepy. By nine-thirty she'd given up and gone to bed.

So now she was stuck with doing the rest. Taking down the art, rehanging around the Tennisson and then getting herself back to the office the moment she finished up. Not all the gallery had to be finished today, but she'd learned not to put off too many things until the last minute.

Mr. Scott had been understanding when she'd explained that the delivery men were due this morning, and she had to be on hand to let them in and sign a receipt, but he'd reminded her rather pointedly that the extensions were due out at the end of the week.

Lu finished stripping the walls. Arnold B. Tennisson had better be worth all this extra work. At the museum's suggestion, and her own expense, she'd even attached a rider to her insurance policy for the month it would be on loan. The only thing she refused to do was give up one of her two free half days a week.

While she waited, she double-checked the security system she'd had installed six years before when she'd first begun fulfilling Andrew's dream of housing a gallery for regional art in their home.

Poor Andrew. He would have had half a dozen of the county's top art students to help him, plus a reporter and a photographer to record the whole process. Meanwhile, perched on his stool, looking distinguished and handsome in his favorite black turtleneck and beige cords, he would have delivered a witty and informative lecture on the proper way to hang a wall.

Andrew had envisioned the gallery being open daily, with discussion groups and poetry readings and traveling exhibitions—all sorts of refinements that Lu had not been able to manage on her own. As he'd spent every cent he could accumulate on acquiring his collection, she'd been left practically destitute at his unexpected death.

Her linen slacks snagged on a splinter on the ladder, and she muttered under her breath. Image be damned—one of these days she was going to give up trying to live up to this damned mausoleum of a house and her lofty position as keeper of the Culhane-Lavender flame and dress the way she wanted to!

Andrew had been slated for a statewide post in the arts when he'd had his first and final heart attack. Before he'd been dead a week, the town of Parrish Falls—where Lavenders and Culhanes had lived since they'd first stolen the land from the Indians—had commissioned an enormous granite monument with a bronze plaque to grace the front yard of the Victorian house that had been built by some ancestor or other— she could never remember if it was the one who'd made the best moonshine in three counties or the one who'd been the governor back in the early part of the century.

At Andrew's death, Lu had been left with no money, few marketable skills, and the burden of carrying out her late husband's dying wish. The citizens had spent all they felt they could afford on the monument. To Lu they'd offered a wealth of advice on matters of dress, deportment and investments. They'd warned her of the pitfalls lying in wait for any unwary young widow left to fend for herself—and then they'd left her to fend for herself.

The Tennisson arrived while she was perched on the ladder eating a tomato sandwich, trying to keep the juice from running into the sleeves of her pink broadcloth shirt.

"One of these days..." Lu muttered, wiping a smear of mayonnaise from her chin. One of these days she was going to shock her public by dressing in jeans, sneakers and a Micky Mouse T-shirt to deliver her little piece on the effects of Culhane County, North Carolina, on the international art scene.

The front door opened, and two men in coveralls entered. So much for her security system; she'd forgotten to switch it on after she'd checked it. "You Miz Lavender? Got a crate for you—weighs a ton. Sign here, okay?"

Lu scrambled down, leaving half a soggy sandwich on top of the ladder. She signed, directed and prevailed on the men to unscrew the lid of the enormous crate. She could have managed it herself, but she would just as soon not take the risk of dropping it. They not only unscrewed the lid, but they also removed the bubble-wrapped canvas and propped it against the wall in the designated spot and then took the crate and lid down to the basement storage room.

"Would you like a tomato sandwich and a glass of iced tea?" she asked when they trooped back upstairs, mopping sweaty foreheads. The air conditioning did not extend to the attic or the basement. "They're my own homegrown tomatoes."

They accepted the tea, declined the sandwiches and strolled around the room, commenting at length on the various paintings. Lu agreed with most of their rather pithy remarks.

After they left, she confronted the Tennisson canvas. It was titled *Hegemony*, and in parentheses beneath the NFS designation on the label, which meant it was not for sale, the value was listed for insurance purposes.

"Oh, dear heavenly days," Lu said in awed tones. It was valued at more than the rest of the collection put together, with her car and a few acres of prime bottom land thrown in for good measure.

And it was *ugly*! Surely not even Andrew could have rationalized four by six feet of scraggly pink and maroon stripes and blotches on a muddy black background, all framed in what looked like flattened chrome bumpers. There was no way it was going to fit into even the largest of the three rooms that had been turned over to the gallery—not without taking over completely.

Maybe if she gave it a room all to itself—the attic, for instance....

Oh, well, what did she know about art? She'd been an agronomy major before she'd dropped out of school to marry Andrew. He'd taught her all she knew about art when she would much rather have been working outside. Given a choice of duties after they were married, she would have preferred plowing, fertilizing and landscaping every available square foot of civic soil in Parish Falls.

Only she hadn't been given a choice. She'd loved Andrew—she'd even understood his passion for encouraging the appreciation of art at the earliest possible age—but there were times when she wished he'd never whispered that last impassioned plea.

"My gallery, Tallulah—promise me you'll do it for me," he'd urged, and she'd promised. She would have promised him her life at that moment if he'd asked.

Sometimes it seemed as if the effect had been the same.

By the time she finished getting the thing hung and surrounded it with the largest and boldest of Andrew's collection the office was closed. She would simply have to go in early tomorrow and stay late to make up for it. She put away the tools, the ladder and the half-eaten sandwich. There was still that thick packet of information to study. It had arrived a week ago, and she'd been putting off digging into it. The bio and credits she could post in the foyer under the sign announcing the special showing, but she needed to go over the other junk several times to be able to discuss the man's work with any degree of intelligence.

If a picture was worth a thousand words, she asked herself as she dumped the fat manila folder into her cluttered desk, why did she have to have the thousand words along with it? Suffice it to say that Arnold B. Tennisson was a semilocal artist who had gone to New York and made good—made exceptionally good, in fact. His first show had sold out, and he now had works in major collections on three continents.

Whether he could conquer Parrish Falls remained to be seen.

It was late by the time Lu was ready to turn off the gallery lights and go upstairs to her own portion of the house, now crowded with generations of Culhane and Lavender furniture that she didn't quite dare dispose of. She was bone tired, sick of art and, as usual, feeling trapped and resentful and guilty about both feelings. For the sake of her mental health, it was a good thing that the Leonards, who had bought the farm after her grandfather's death, were both generous and understanding. One more day and a half and she would be able to drive out to the pond, where she could laze away an entire afternoon being completely unproductive and as slovenly as she pleased with no one around to criticize.

Playing lady was damned hard work for someone who'd grown up wearing bib overalls and thick-soled boots.

Lu's mind took off on a tangent as she thought about the last time she'd been out at the pond. Who *was* this Rex Jones fellow? What was he doing around here? There'd been something on the door of his van, but for the life of her, she couldn't recall what it was. A business of some sort? He was probably a delivery man or a repairman. Power Plant Road was off the beaten track, some four miles from town. There was nothing out that way except the farm and the power plant. Maybe he had something to do with the new milking machines Gus Leonard had recently installed.

The thunderstorm waited until noon on Wednesday, her half day off from the office. Lu barely got home before it cut loose, blasting everything in sight. She wasn't exactly afraid of lightning, but she had better sense than to go fishing in a thunderstorm. Instead she curled up on the horsehair sofa and spent the afternoon with a paperback thriller. August was turning out to be a record breaker when it came to heat and thunderstorms.

Friday afternoon Lu left work early to stop by the post office before it closed. She had a stack of extended tax returns to send by certified mail that needed to be postmarked today.

She hadn't counted on there being a line. She fidgeted, and when Lu fidgeted, she invariably got the hiccups. It always happened when she was anxious. The door opened, and more people joined the line, shuffling and speaking in undertones. Her next-door neighbor, Lana Potts, was taking forever to make up her mind which stamps she wanted—the ones with the fish or the ones with Enrico Caruso.

The late-afternoon sun baked through the plate-glass window, and she hiccupped and tugged at the waist of her blue-and-white striped dress. She had on too many clothes. Even a single layer was too much on a day like this. She could've gotten by without a slip. The hair she'd French braided this morning was frayed, with loose strands tickling her face and neck, and her thighs had begun to itch from her panty hose before she'd walked two blocks.

From his vantage point in the line, Rex watched the woman squirm, shift her weight and hiccup. The first few times, she'd begged the pardon of everyone in general, but after that, she appeared to be trying to make herself smaller.

He smiled. Everyone in line was smiling. The back of her neck was pink, plastered with small dark curls. He'd seen hair like that only recently, but instead of being piled up into a sophisticated doohickey on top of a regal little head, it had been crammed under a yellow duckbill hat.

"That time o' year again, right, Miz Lavender? First it's April fifteenth, then come the extensions. Back in my day, it was always March." The comment came from the man directly in front of him, and Rex waited to see if she would turn around. It couldn't be the same woman, of course, but there was something about her...

She turned around. Her reply was lost on Rex, because he was struck by the most perfect profile he'd ever had the good fortune to see. It was either the same woman or she had a twin sister stashed out in the country. He hoped to hell it was the latter, because he didn't much like the sound of that "Miz Lavender" business. What was the good of finding the woman of your dreams if she'd already been found by someone else first?

Hiccup! "I'm sorry, Mr. Timmons. I always do that when I'm nervous, and I'm afraid the window will close before I can get these postmarked, and you know the IRS. They're not going to want to hear about Mrs. Potts and her stamps and about all the envelopes being stuck together on account of the humidity."

And then, to Rex's amazement, her gaze moved beyond her friend, and he found himself staring down at her like a thunderstruck idiot. She smiled at him. The cavern that opened in his chest could have swallowed up the entire state of Rhode Island, no problem.

"Oh, hello—it's Mr. Jones, isn't it?" She hiccupped and touched her lips apologetically.

It took a while before Rex could synchronize brain and tongue enough to reply. ''Yes, ma'am. Not fishing today, uh—Mrs. Lavender?''

''Not today, Mr. Jones'' was all she said, but it was enough. The line moved forward and split as another window opened, and before Rex could come up with another brilliant observation, she was engaged in filling out forms.

Talk about filling out forms!

He was third in line when she left. After watching her out of sight, he turned back to the man in front of him. Simmons? Turner? What the dickens had she called him, anyway? This was his chance to find out more about her, possibly the only chance he would get, but without arousing suspicion, he could hardly tap the guy on the shoulder and ask for a rundown on the beautiful woman who'd just walked out. He was, after all, a stranger in town. And it would seem that she was a married woman.

''You a friend o' Miz Lavender's?'' Turner-Simmons inquired, taking in everything from Rex's booted feet to his creased khakis and his sweat-stained shirt to the top of his shaggy, sun-bleached hair.

Giving thanks to providence for the curiosity of small-town residents for any newcomer in their midst, Rex replied, ''We've only met a couple of times. She seems like a nice enough woman.'' He'd gauged the man's propensity for gossip to within a few microns. Now he waited.

''Oh, they don't come much finer than Lu Lavender. I was telling Hector Perryman just this morning that she turned out to be a real credit to the Lavender

name, even if some said she *was* too young to take on
so much responsibility after Andrew passed on, and
Hector, he said to me—"

"Next?"

The man stepped up to the window, and Rex restrained himself forcibly from spinning him around
and demanding to know what the hell Hector had
said. By the time he'd bought a stamp and slipped
Chloe's monthly rent check into the out-of-state slot,
along with a note assuring her he would get in touch
with the small Delaware power plant that had written
twice and called three times, Simmons-Turner was
gone.

Did the passing on of this Andrew guy mean that
she was a widow? Was it a mortal sin to hope so? Because splitting up a happily married couple was against
his principles, but if she was still married, they were all
in a heap of trouble. One way or another, Rex was
going to get her.

He closed his mind to all the reasons why he hadn't
a snowball's chance in hell of succeeding.

Two

Lu was still smiling when she reached home, in spite of the heat, in spite of her chafed thighs, in spite of the thought of tomorrow's duty as hostess, caretaker and resident lecturer at the Andrew C. Lavender Memorial Gallery of Art.

What an odd man. What an *intriguing* man. He was far from handsome, with those raw, forceful features, and yet there was something almost compelling about him.

Yes—that was it. Compelling, in an unexpected way. There was a quality of latent sensuality about him that was totally unexpected, possibly because his manner was so disarming. He could have been a Viking explorer or the original Marlboro man. His hair, sun-bleached to the color of straw, was straight, slightly shaggy and looked as if would take at least a hay rake to tame it. Although *tame* was hardly a word she would ever have associated with Rex Jones.

Oddly enough, she'd trusted him instinctively the first time she'd ever seen him. And Lu was no push-over. She'd been warned too often about trusting strange men.

Still smiling, she let herself into the house, grateful for the climate-control system she'd been forced to install for the protection of Andrew's art collection. Often, when she felt like chucking the whole business and doing something wild and totally impractical, she reminded herself of all the benefits to be had from sharing her home with a public art collection. Air conditioning, an excellent burglar system...

A complete lack of privacy.

One of these days she was probably going to give in to temptation and let Hector Perryman take over part of her duties. He'd started hinting at some such ar-rangement the moment he'd discovered that she was planning to carry on with Andrew's dream of a local gallery where people could see what was being pro-duced in their own part of the country.

Poor Hector. She'd given him a subtle brush-off— evidently a bit too subtle, for he'd persisted, remind-ing her that he'd been considered the authority in Culhane County on all things artistic at a time when Andrew had been merely a high school art teacher who occasionally was asked to judge the art exhibits at the county fair.

It had been more than six years since Andrew had died, Lu realized with something of a start. Some-times it seemed like six days; sometimes it seemed like forever. For more than half the eleven years they'd been married, he'd talked about the gallery he wanted to create.

Poor old Hector, whose occasional stilted little art critiques vied for space in the *Culhane County Courier* with all the church, farm bureau and club news, had taken potshots at Andrew in every column. Andrew had been just as bad, deliberately undermining Hector's authority at every opportunity.

Lu honestly wasn't sure whether she continued to hold out against asking for Hector's help because she didn't like him personally or because of the silly feud between the two men. In her weaker moments she wanted nothing so much as to walk out and lock the door behind her and get a job doing something she enjoyed, something that didn't require her to keep up appearances. As it was, she was growing old devoting all her energies to two demanding jobs, neither of which gave her very much satisfaction.

The phone rang before she could even get her clothes off. For one brief moment as she raced across the room in her stocking feet, she entertained the idea that it might be Rex Jones. But that was silly—he didn't even know her name, much less where she lived.

It was Hector. "You've hung that abomination, haven't you? I saw the delivery truck and watched the men carry in a big crate. Tallulah, didn't I warn you about Arnold Tennisson? The man's a charlatan."

"Mr. Perryman, I know you don't care for Tennisson's work, but—"

"*Care* for it! The boy made a name for himself only because he spilled paint on a dirty rag and had the gall to enter it in some trumped-up show. It was a pure case of the emperor's new clothes that the danged thing won! Not a single judge had the gumption to admit that the thing was trash for fear he'd be accused of not understanding it.''

"Mr. Perryman, it's only one canvas. I'm not wild about it, either, and I don't pretend to understand it, but that doesn't make it any less valid.''

"Valid! You sound just like that husband of yours with his fancy phrases, but let me tell you something, my dear young lady, fancy words don't turn garbage into gold any more than—''

"I'm sorry, Mr. Perryman, but I really do have to go now.'' She hung up, feeling guilty and small-minded because she'd been brusque to a frustrated old man whose ego Andrew had consistently deflated.

Tossing her clothes across a wicker table in her up-stairs sitting room, she'd managed to peel down to her pantyhose and bra when the doorbell sounded. She swore softly. If that old worrywart had come around to try to make her take the Tennisson down, she was going to let him have it with both barrels. No more Mrs. Nice Guy!

The buzzer sounded again, long and hard. Muttering threats, Lu pulled on her dress, hastily buttoning it as she hurried down the stairs in her stocking feet.

"Mr. Perryman—Mr. *Jones*? What are *you* doing here?''

If Rex had been in the habit of wearing a hat, it would have been in his hands. His whole attitude was one of apology mixed with dogged determination.

"Miz Lavender, ma'am, I was told you operate a gallery on the premises."

Miz Lavender, ma'am, I wuz told you operate a bordello on the premises. Lu struggled to keep a straight face. This had all the earmarks of one of grandpop's favorite old TV westerns. "Well, yes, but it's not—"

"I thought if it was all the same to you, ma'am, I'd just have me a look-see. Got a friend about to graduate from medical school, and I thought a picture might make a right nice graduation present."

"It's Texas, isn't it?" she blurted out, suddenly placing the accent. Not only the dialect, but the words. Come to think of it, even the physical characteristics were right on target. Rex Jones could easily have doubled for one of those tall, tough hombres who rode into town on a mean-looking horse, his hat pulled low over his eyes and his gun belt slung low on his hips. Grandpop would have adored him!

Rex nodded. "Yes'm, I'm from down Galveston way." Now that he was here, he wondered where he'd parked his brains. It was one thing to walk up to a good-looking woman in a bar and strike up a conversation. It was another thing altogether with a woman like Lu Lavender. Somehow, no matter what he said, it was going to sound like a line. Hell, it *was* a line!

He was still studying the toe of his boot when she said with a hint of regret, "Mr. Jones, the Andrew C. Lavender Memorial Gallery is open to the public between the hours of ten and six on Saturdays and one and five on Sunday afternoons. I'm sorry if you've come all this way for nothing, but we aren't a selling gallery, at any rate. I could give you the names of several artists in the area if you'd like to contact them personally.''

Why hadn't she taken time to put on her shoes, at least? She was a good five feet five, but this was like trying to converse with Mount Rushmore. He made her feel all sorts of things she wasn't really comfortable feeling. Like small. Like vulnerable.

Like extremely and essentially female.

"Oh."

How was it possible to wrap so much disappointment into a single word? It must have been that raspy drawl of his. It must have been the heat. It must have been a sudden attack of some mysterious force that struck down lonely young widows in the prime of life.

"I'm downright sorry to have bothered you, ma'am. See, the thing is, I don't know a whole lot about art and it occurred to me that you might be able to, uh, give me a few pointers on what to look for. In a picture, that is. I'd hate to send Max and Chloe something they'd be embarrassed to have in their house.''

Lu felt herself beginning to weaken. It was not merely the fact that the man had such an engagingly diffident smile. It certainly wasn't the fact that his eyes crinkled at the corners in such a way that she felt almost compelled to smile back. She *did* have her civic duty to consider. He *was* a newcomer, after all. And he was looking for a painting. And like it or not, she did happen to run the town's only art gallery.

"Look, Mr. Jones, I—"

"I'd appreciate it if you'd make that Rex, ma'am. I'm a stranger around these parts, and to tell you the truth, a man gets downright lonesome for the sound of a friendly voice speaking his name. But then, I don't suppose you'd know about that, being as everybody in town has a kind word to say for Miz Lavender.''

Oops, Rex thought—tactical error. Now she would think he'd been prying behind her back when the truth was he'd only mentioned her to the postmaster and the man who'd been in front of him in line. He'd caught up with Turner-Simmons—whose name turned out to be Timmons—at the Shell station, and they'd chatted while they'd pumped gas.

It had been a good thing he had an oversize tank in the van. By the time he'd filled it to capacity at the slowest speed at which the pump would operate, he'd learned that Tallulah Stevens had grown up on the old Stevens farm that was now the Leonard farm out on Power Plant Road, and had set the town on its heels by marrying a guy named Lavender, the only son of the local landed gentry, to the dismay of every available female between Deep Gap, Pipers Gap and Roaring Gap.

He'd learned that poor Lavender had been called from this vale of tears at an unduly early age, leaving his poor widow in possession of as fine a piece of real estate as could be found anywhere in Culhane County, much to the chagrin of an elderly cousin over Elkin way, who thought that a Stevens, being only fourth-generation Culhane County, had no business being in possession of such a historic treasure.

Oh, yes, Rex had had an earful, all right.

And now he had an eyeful. The truth was, if she was fourth generation or first, he was way out of his league. She was something special, this lady of the floppy green sneakers and the starchy little manners. There was something about her that was making his brain seize up like an overheated engine. He hadn't been in this bad a shape since he was fifteen years old.

Lu waited for him to go or stay—or at least say something. He seemed to have forgotten what he was doing there. With a look of resignation, she swung wide the door and invited him in. "Look, officially we're closed, but as long as you're here I suppose you might as well come on in for a few minutes." Since he seemed to have taken root on her front porch, it was either that or shove him down the steps and out onto the sidewalk, and she had an idea that Rex Jones didn't shove easily.

He followed her inside with that hat-in-hand air that seemed so out of place in a man of his stature, waiting while she switched on the track lights in the three-room gallery. "I'm impressed," he said quietly, the drawl not quite so pronounced.

"I'm glad. Look as long you want to. Now if you'll excuse me . . ." Lu turned toward the stairs that led to her private living quarters on the second floor, anxious to get away from the man who disturbed her in a way she didn't quite understand.

"Hey, you're not leaving me on my own here, are you?" Rex didn't give damn about the paintings—it was the woman he was interested in. Only now that he was here, he wasn't sure how to go about dealing with a respectable widow when his intentions were anything *but* respectable.

Startled, Lu glanced back. Was that panic she detected in his voice? What the dickens was going on here? First he wanted in, then he wanted out! By his own statement, Rex Jones didn't know the first thing about art. Why not simply buy his friend a nice coffee-table book or a solid brass cuspidor and let it go at that?

"I'll be back in a minute," she said more gently than she might have. She was bone tired and hungry, and she hadn't even had time to change her clothes. "Go ahead, look around. As I said before, I know some of the artists personally, so if you see anything you particularly like, perhaps I can arrange something."

Moments later, she leaned her warm forehead against the cool mirror over the bathroom basin. Whew! What was it they said about women in their late thirties? They were at their peak of sexual something-or-other?

With a man like Rex Jones around, she could well believe it! He hadn't been the least bit forward—there'd been no sign at all of any interest in her as a woman, yet she'd reacted the same way she used to when Andrew had smiled at her in a certain way and lifted one eyebrow, nodding toward the stairs.

Only in this case, there'd been no slow, familiar warmup period. Without even knowing her burner had been switched on, she'd suddenly come to a full rolling boil!

This must be what some of the more veiled warnings had been about—all those knowing whispers about a woman's needs, about the problems that arise when a woman who's been used to having a man around is suddenly left alone. She'd thought they meant something else entirely, and she'd easily shrugged them off. Having grown up on a farm, she was as handy with tools as most men—handier than some. Andrew, for instance, hadn't even known how to change a fuse, much less a spark plug.

A little defiantly, Lu dressed in jeans and a yellow cotton pullover and tugged her dark hair back into a ponytail. For good measure, she scrubbed off what little makeup hadn't already melted, leaving her face pink and shining. That should discourage him, she thought, and then her shoulders slumped.

It wasn't Rex Jones who needed discouraging, she reminded herself. He'd still been at the "yes ma'am, thank you ma'am" stage when she'd been fighting the urge to check the curve of his muscles under the trim-fitting khakis.

"Oh, Lordy, I'm losing touch with reality," she muttered.

"Miz Lavender? You in here?" With no more than a perfunctory rap on her partially opened door, Rex stuck his head inside, managing to grin and look apologetic at the same time. "Sorry to keep bothering you, ma'am."

The man was talented, she had to admit. With a terseness that was only partially due to irritation, Lu said, "Mr. Jones, this part of the house is off limits to the public!"

"Yes'm, I sorta thought so, but you see, I had a question, and I was afraid you wouldn't come back downstairs in time. I did call from the bottom landing, but I reckon you didn't hear me, what with the air conditioner going full blast."

A likely story, Jones. She was beginning to suspect that Rex Jones wasn't quite as guileless as he appeared to be. "I told you I'd be back down. You should have waited. What's your question?"

"My question?" He still stood in the doorway of her upstairs sitting room, looking totally alien amid the feminine clutter.

"You said you had a question about one of the paintings," she reminded him.

"Uh, not exactly. Not about a painting, I mean. You see, like I said, I'm new in town, ma'am, and I was wondering if you might know a decent place to eat. I've been staying out at the Peacock Motel near the interstate, but the food's not much good. Fact is, I don't think I can face another meal there."

Lu reached out to steady herself on a round wicker table, and her fingers brushed against the slip she'd discarded earlier. She hastily brushed it onto the floor and kicked it under a chaise longue. It had been six years since a man had entered this room, and this one took up entirely too much space. "Oh. Well...there's Bart and Mamie's. The country ham and vegetables are great, but I can't say much for the desserts."

"Oh, well now, I'm a man who likes desserts."

Lu's gaze skimmed his trim waistline—not an inch of excess weight—and swallowed hard. "Look, why don't we go back downstairs?" She practically shoved

him from the room before she remembered that she
still wasn't wearing any shoes. Never mind—the important thing was to get him out of there. "Adam's
Truck Stop has the best chicken-fried steak, and their
cobblers are great, too. They're easy to find—you just
go all the way out toward highway eighteen as if you
were—"

"What about their vegetables?" Rex murmured
absently. Funny—he'd never particularly noticed a
woman's fingernails before. Unless they were fire-
engine red, which sort of put him off. She had the
prettiest fingernails he'd ever seen. They were a perfect size, a perfect shape, a perfect color.

He halted on the bottom step and turned to look up
at her, two steps behind and above him. Their eyes
were on a level, and Lu found her gaze getting tangled up in the most ridiculously long, sun-tipped eye-
lashes she'd ever seen on anyone, man or woman.
"I'm afraid they're mostly canned," she whispered.

His eyes were neither green nor brown, but a mix-
ture that was too complex to be called plain hazel. He
narrowed them, and Lu felt a rise of goose bumps
along her flanks. This was absurd! The man was new
in town, he asked about restaurants, and suddenly her
knees were wobbling and she couldn't catch her
breath! That corned-beef-and-cucumber sandwich for
lunch had been a mistake; she should have known
better.

"Tell you what, Miz Lavender, if you wouldn't
mind doing me a big favor, maybe you'd go along with
me to one of those places—maybe the chicken-fried
steak and cobbler place. Long's I have somebody to

talk to, I don't mind about canned vegetables. I guess
it's just being alone so much that gets to a guy after a
while."

"Mr. Jones, I don't—"

"Of course, I'm not dressed up fancy or anything.
And we haven't been properly introduced. I'm sorry,
Miz Lavender, I shouldn't have insulted you by ask-
ing you out like that. I just wasn't thinking. Selfish,
that's what I am—plain selfish. Comes of living alone,
I reckon."

"Oh, please—don't apologize. I mean, it's all right.
You certainly haven't insulted me. I should thank you
for your invitation."

His face brightened. "You mean you will?"

"No," she said softly, regretfully. "I'm afraid I
can't, but it was nice of you to ask. And do try
Adam's Truck Stop. I think you'll like it."

The moment he'd left she felt like calling him back
and offering to cook his supper, which made her feel
like even more of an idiot. Some third-rate cowboy
whose charm was about as genuine as a three-dollar
diamond spins out a line, and she blithely trips over it!
As if she couldn't recognize a philanderer when she
met one. In retrospect, at least.

How could any woman her age be so *dense*? It must
have something to do with his size. Andrew had been
a rather small man, and she just wasn't accustomed to
being in close quarters with so much...with such a...

Well, with whatever it was. He radiated it. Two
minutes inside her private sitting room and he'd practically created a storm center! And then, when he'd
backed out again, he'd left such a gaping hole in the

atmosphere that she'd actually felt the currents of air raising goose bumps on her arms.

Dammit, the man had barged in where he had no business barging. She should have called the police, and instead she'd actually considered going out with him. For just a moment. Before her better judgment had intervened.

She wandered out to the kitchen, opened the refrigerator door and stared at the contents. What was she going to fix for supper? What had he thought of that Tennisson abomination? Had he looked at the paintings at all, or had it only been an excuse?

With an exasperated sigh, she closed the door again, sat down at the table and frowned at the tops of the overgrown shrubbery that ran along the southeast side of the house. She'd overfertilized a few years ago in an excess of zeal, and had been too busy to cut them back ever since. At the rate she was wasting time they would be over the gutters in another few years!

And just as if she didn't have enough on her mind, with this Tennisson exhibit and all, along came this cowboy to set her hormones jangling with his chipped-tooth grin and his crinkly eyes.

Plus a few other goodies, a wicked little voice reminded her.

If she were brutally honest, Lu knew she'd wanted to believe that the painting for a friend had only been an excuse to see her again. Unfortunately it didn't add up.

Oh, sure, after checking over her stock to see if she had something his friend might be interested in, he'd asked her out to dinner, but he'd taken no for an an-

swer awfully quickly. And come to think of it, he
hadn't said anything about meeting any of the artists
who sold from their studios, either.

Okay, so he wasn't interested in the art and he
wasn't interested in her. What *was* he interested in?

Her gaze swung slowly to the Tennisson. Surely he
wasn't— No. That was ridiculous. The man was no art
thief—she would bank on that. It would take a lot of
panache to walk out of here with a four-by-six-foot
monstrosity framed in chrome tucked under his arm,
and Rex Jones was about as unsophisticated as they
came.

A little too unsophisticated, perhaps? Come to
think of it, he'd spread it on pretty thick—the grits-
and-gravy school of charm. Maybe he'd wanted to
disarm her, to deflect her suspicions. He could have
had no way of knowing that far from being suspicious, she'd been so unexpectedly turned on that she'd
practically blown a fuse before she could hustle him
out of her house.

In no better frame of mind than before, Lu locked
the front door, checked the other two doors and set the
alarm system. If it ever went off, she would probably
go through the roof, but to get insurance, she'd had to
have it. That done, she spread herself a peanut butter
sandwich and poured a glass of milk. She would take
them upstairs and watch whatever movie was on TV
tonight. She only hoped it wasn't a western!

Saturday morning got off to a bad start when Lu
broke a nail, spilled dusting powder all over the bathroom floor and popped runs in two new pairs of panty

hose. Feeling more than a little frazzled, she opened the front door to greet the gallery's first two visitors.

Rex and Hector. They were eying each other with mutual distrust, but Rex stepped back and allowed the older man to enter first.

"Tallulah, I hope you've had time enough to reconsider exhibiting that awful piece of trash." As usual, Hector smelled of mothballs and mouthwash. "Just because it was available for loan, that's no reason for the people of Culhane County to lower their standards."

"Tallulah?" Rex repeated softly. "Isn't that an Indian name?"

"I haven't the faintest idea. I was named after my mother, and she was named after a waterfall. Did you come back to look for something for your friend, after all?"

"No, ma'am, I came to look for something for myself."

"It's an abomination," Hector went on, his shiny pink scalp catching the reflection of the track lighting as he turned to glare at the depressing canvas.

"The chicken-fried steak was great, and so was the peach cobbler, but it was awful lonesome with nothing but a plastic posey and a bottle of catsup for company," Rex said softly.

Lu turned from one to the other of the two men. She felt besieged. When the door opened and the summer art honors group from the local junior high shoved in, snickering and elbowing one another, she felt an overwhelming sense of relief. Kids she could handle. Even Hector she could deal with if she had to, but this tall Texan was another matter altogether. He wasn't even looking at the paintings, but was smiling down at her in a way that brought heat rising to her cheeks.

He listened to every word she said, even when she repeated herself for different groups. He listened when she stumbled, and by the time he'd been there all morning, she was stumbling quite badly.

"Would you please stop doing that?" she whispered furiously when she found herself alone in the small gallery with him. She snatched up a bubble gum wrapper someone had tucked behind the corner of a frame.

"Stop looking at the pictures?"

"Stop harassing me!"

No angel could have looked more innocent. "Ma'am, if I'm bothering you, it's surely not my intention. I only—"

"Oh . . . stuff it, Jones!" Unwilling to fight with someone who refused to fight fair, she spun away, but not before she caught the twitch at the corner of his lips.

The wretch! With both the temperature and the humidity at a comfortable low, she was steaming hot and her hair was sticking to the back of her neck. And he actually had the gall to stand there *grinning*!

Rex left soon after that. As usual, Hector stayed on. So far, he'd outlasted two summer art honors groups, three couples who'd driven over from Roaring Gap and the few locals who wandered in to take advantage of the air conditioning.

Lu sensed that he was just waiting to get her alone. He obviously had something more to say on the subject of the Tennisson, and she didn't want to hear it.

She wasn't given the option. "I suppose you think those children benefited from seeing tripe like that displayed as though it had some great social significance," Hector accused, catching her just as she said goodbye to two retired school teachers. "Next thing you know, they'll all be splashing paint on anything that comes to hand and calling it great art. You'll rue the day, my dear child—take my word for it. You've done Parrish Falls a great disservice by going along with those liberals who are out to destroy this great land of ours with just such tactics."

Lu's shoulders sagged. "Hector, I don't like the thing any more than you do, but I fail to see how exhibiting a painting can destroy a country. The kids made fun of it, in case you didn't notice. They made fun of Agatha Lennon's primitive, too, and that's certainly American enough, isn't it?" Which probably meant that she wasn't doing a very good job of interpreting, she thought tiredly.

"You're an intelligent woman, Tallulah. Don't tell me you missed the significance of those stars and stripes."

"Stars and stripes? You can't mean all those wiggly lines and blotches."

"The man's subtle, I'll give him that. Pink instead of red. Humph! Well, I'm not so easily hoodwinked, I'll tell you that much. I know a left-wing painting when I see one, you mark my words."

Lu felt her jaw drop. Surely he couldn't be serious? Dear Lord, he was! Poor old Hector, seeing ghosts and goblins behind every door. If it weren't so pathetic, it might be funny. "I grant you, the thing's ugly, Hector," she said gently. "But that's no crime. It's probably the only reason we were able to get it from the museum's loan program—no one else wanted to borrow it."

"You made a grave mistake, Tallulah. You simply don't have the background to understand the meaning of art."

She couldn't argue that fact. She'd married Andrew, not his life's dream. "Hector, if you don't mind, I'm going to slip out to the kitchen and have a bite to eat while there's no one here."

"I'll stay and keep an eye on things for you, my dear. Take your time, take your time," the sweating little man in the rumpled white suit said, and Lu groaned inwardly. That wasn't what she'd meant at all. She might've known he wouldn't take the hint.

"Thanks. It's not at all necessary, but thanks."

Hector left shortly after two, with another doleful look at the offending work, and Lu went through her spiel for three sets of visitors and the mailman, who happened to think the Tennisson was super. It reminded him of his early days as a crop duster, he said—rows and rows of muddy fields with small blotches of whatever crop happened to be growing. It seemed that one of the pesticides he'd used took on a mauve cast once it was spread over green.

"It's all in the eye of the beholder," she said, showing him out, and then her own eyes beheld a familiar van pulling up under the shade of the tulip poplar.

He was back again. Lu didn't even want to think about how glad she was to see him—it was too disconcerting.

Grinning broadly, Rex Jones strode toward her, looking like some storybook version of a conquering hero as the lowering sun cast a bronze glow over his angular features. She was still standing in the doorway when he took the granite steps two at a time. "Evening, Miz Lavender. Say, d'you mind if I call you Tallulah?"

"I prefer Lu," she said, her voice only slightly breathless. "Did you forget and leave something here earlier, Mr. Jones?"

"Why no, ma'am. The fact is, Lu, I owe you a favor, and I'm a man who insists on paying his debts."

What he owed her was an apology and an explanation, and a fast goodbye, she thought with a partial return to sanity. The trouble was, whenever she looked at that face of his, all her common sense seemed to fly right out the window.

Almost with a sense of relief, she stepped aside to allow him to enter. Her eyes closed briefly as she inhaled the masculine scent of his body. He smelled clean, like soap and sun-warmed skin, with a hint of some woodsy fragrance. His khakis were crisp, his boots polished and his hair looked as if he'd at least made an attempt to control it. An unsuccessful attempt.

"A favor?" she repeated. After she'd all but invited him to leave this afternoon, she had hardly expected him to show up at all, much less in such a generous mood.

He reached behind her to close the door, and his hand happened to close over her own. *Be still my foolish heart,* Lu warned silently, reminding herself that she was a mature woman with a responsible position in the community. Unfortunately all the circuits between her brain and her body seemed to have been disconnected.

"The fact is, ma'am, that place you steered me to last night was a sight better than the restaurant out at the motel. I do appreciate your kindness, ma'am. To repay you, I insist on taking you out to dinner tonight."

"Oh, but—"

"Hush now, Lu—I owe you a favor, and I'll be plumb miserable if you don't let me pay you back. You wouldn't want that on your conscience, would you?"

The guilelessness of his expression was so at odds with the ruggedness of his features—and with the twinkle in those deep-set eyes of his—that she had to laugh. "I think I've been set up."

"I'm trying my best, ma'am," he replied with a grin that tilted one corner of his mouth.

"Could we dispense with the Texas blarney?"

"Well, now that's a right tall order. I'll try, though, if that's the way you want it, ma'am."

"Cut it, Mr. Jones."

"Right, Mrs. Lavender."

Taking the line of least resistance, Lu relented. She leaned her back against the burlap-covered wall, crossing her arms over her chest, and studied him openly. "Rex, level with me—what's this all about, anyway? Are you an art thief?"

He looked stunned. "A *what* thief?"

She nodded to the Tennisson in the room beyond. "That's the only thing in the collection worth more than a couple of thousand. It was right about the time it was scheduled to arrive that you and your van started turning up everywhere I looked. If it's the painting you're after, I might as well warn you, it's wired directly to the police station with a hidden fool-proof switch." Which was a slight exaggeration, but she hoped he wouldn't know it.

Rex turned to consider the thing on the far wall. Feet spread apart, he rocked back on his heels, scratched his jaw and then turned back to face the small woman with the beautiful, if belligerent, gray eyes. "Ma'am, you'll pardon me for saying so, but I wouldn't hit a dog in the, uh, rump with that thing. To tell you the truth, I just want to get to know you."

He wanted to get to *know* her? There were several degrees of "knowing." Lu's mind boggled at the pos-sibilities. "Oh. Okay then," she said a bit warily. "If that's all you want, I suppose I could have dinner with you."

Of course she'd never *seriously* considered the pos-sibility that he might be a crook. Not really, she told herself. Even with all his southern-fried charm, he was an unmistakable example of a classic good-guy type. She recognized him immediately, even without the white hat.

"Well, now, I'm not saying that's all I want," Rex teased, his deep, raspy voice raising havoc with her system. "It'll do to start with, though."

Lu sagged against the wall, hoping he couldn't see the effect his words had on her. Unfortunately dinner wasn't all she wanted from him, either. It was all she dared accept, though, and even at that she was probably taking a risk.

Whew! Suddenly she felt as if she were coming down with a fever. She felt almost giddy—as if she'd done something daring and more than a little bit dangerous, when the truth was, she'd merely accepted a dinner invitation.

The trouble was, she'd been cooped up in this claustrophobic atmosphere too long. Too much righteousness and rectitude tended to make a woman fanciful, she rationalized. Rex had no more intention of getting involved with her than she did with him— though that statement didn't bear much scrutiny.

Three

Instead of Adam's Truck Stop, Rex drove them to the most exclusive restaurant in the area. It was fairly new, and Lu had never been there before for the simple reason that she'd never been invited. It wasn't the sort of place a woman went alone, especially not a woman whose modest salary was usually stretched to the limit.

They pulled into the parking lot, and he leaned across her and removed something from the glove compartment. "Will this do, or do you want to take a chance on the establishment's taste in neckties?"

The tie was a plain black wool. With his khakis, it would have the look of a uniform. "It looks fine to me. Is it required?"

"I expect so." He buttoned his collar and knotted the tie, jutting his chin.

There was something incredibly intimate about the small action, and Lu suddenly felt as if she'd stepped off the edge of her safe dull little world into a place that was exciting, if a bit frightening. "The truck stop would've been fine," she murmured.

Ignoring her perfunctory protest, he said, "If I'd known I was going to meet someone like you, I'd have brought along something besides work clothes. I tend to travel light when I'm on a job."

He could have worn a loincloth and looked more magnificent than any other man she'd ever met. Her own yellow-and-white print shirtwaister might look like silk, but it was practical, washable polyester—and six years old, besides.

Rex came around to open her door, and Lu accepted a steadying hand as she slid down from the high seat. Every cell in her body sizzled at his touch. It was all she could do not to gasp when he placed a large warm hand at the small of her back to guide her toward the massive iron-strapped oak door.

The door closed silently behind them, and she stepped closer to his side, gazing around at the discreetly lighted interior. She identified the eucalyptus plant in the corner immediately, if only from pictures. "What a wonderful color," she murmured. "I wonder if I could get a cutting of that to try in my backyard."

"I'm not sure the stuff's even living, but I've got a knife if you really want a chunk. We'll just sort of mosey on over there and back up to the bushes. Better practice lookin' innocent in case we get caught."

Laughing, Lu reached for his hand. "That's really sweet of you, Rex, but I doubt if the city fathers would let me keep it, even if it would grow. They're such sticklers about using only indigenous plants around all the old historic places. But thanks."

"If you're sure." He nodded to a life-size tree made of welded copper and brass nestled among an array of living plants. "I could raid a plumbing supply house and probably find you one of those—or close enough."

"At least that one won't ever shed all over an elegant lobby."

Tucking her hand under his arm, Rex grinned down at her. "Maybe not, but they're so far behind in their mowing—" He indicated the thick silver teal carpet. "This stuff's going to go to seed before they get it baled."

Lu's smile flickered and faded as concern set in. Overhead was something she knew about, and places like this were expensive. Could Rex afford it? Had it even occurred to him that without reservations, they wouldn't stand a chance of being seated? Not for the world would she have him embarrassed. She would rather leave right now, before they were thrown out, and settle for Adam's Truck Stop.

Unconsciously moving closer to his side, Lu shot him a quick glance, noting that he didn't seem the least bit intimidated by his surroundings, in spite of his rather informal garb. In fact, there was something almost arrogant about the easy way he carried himself.

"I'm not looking for trouble, pilgrim, but if it's trouble you want, then I'd be obliged if you'd step outside so we won't mess up the carpet."

Or had it been "upset the ladies"? It had been a long time since she'd thought much about those old western reruns that Grandpop had loved so much. Andrew had despised them.

The maître d' bore down on them, a pained expression on his plump face, and Lu tightened her hand on Rex's arm, feeling fiercely defensive on his behalf. If that overstuffed penguin dared lift one supercilious eyebrow at Rex's khakis and boots, she would personally polish him off, the precious Lavender reputation notwithstanding.

"Ahh, Mr. Jones." It was a statement rather than a question. "We have a very nice table in the grotto, but if you'd prefer the observatory. . . ?"

"The observatory," Lu said quickly. Grotto sounded too much like dungeon, and she refused to be hidden away.

"How did he know who you were?" she whispered as they followed the man to a brass elevator with no visible buttons.

"Beats me. Maybe it was the fact that when I called to tell him we were coming for supper tonight, I mentioned that I had a tie I was willing to wear for a decent cut of beef, but I wouldn't put on a coat in August for a whole Charolais steer."

Lu felt an unholy urge to giggle. She couldn't decide whether Rex was having fun at the expense of the management or merely forcing the world to accept him at his own value. Whatever he was up to, it was obviously working.

And whatever fears she'd harbored in the beginning faded completely as the evening wore on. Rex was a marvelous companion. He knew his beef. He also knew his way around a wine list, and both the waiter and the wine steward, whose French accent had a suspicious Appalachian twang, scurried to do his bidding. Under a star-studded dome, they dined on grilled shrimp, fork-tender cuts of prime beef, tiny cloverleaf rolls and a spinach-and-mushroom salad. Lu devoured the last morsel and looked up to find Rex smiling at her.

"Healthy appetite," he observed.

"Country girl," she explained. Goodness! It had been years since she'd waded into a meal with so much enthusiasm.

"I believe someone mentioned that your folks used to have the place out on Power Plant Road?"

"My grandparents. Actually my father grew up there, but he moved to Raleigh and took a job with the Department of Agriculture. After he and Mama died, I went back to the farm to live." The inquisition was so gentle that she scarcely felt it. Leaning back in her chair, Lu told him about driving a school bus and growing prize-winning cantaloupes, about hay rides and training her grandfather's shoats to sing for their supper.

"We only had a few, and they didn't actually sing, of course, but they always stood up at the fence and squealed the minute they saw me coming with the buckets."

Rex's gaze wandered from her lips to her eyes while she talked. She fascinated him. At times he could have sworn that she was holding back nothing, yet at other times, he'd catch a shadow flickering in the depths of her eyes that made him want to hold her until all the clouds were gone and the sun shone again.

God knows, the last thing he needed in his life was trouble. What he wanted was good times. Good times that didn't depend on yesterdays or tomorrows.

But he couldn't help responding to the laughter, the curiosity, the interest ... and the occasional shadow. He was totally captivated by her small womanly vanities. He was totally captivated by the woman herself, and it was beginning to make him just a tad uneasy.

Signaling quietly for coffee, Rex deflected a question concerning his personal life. He never discussed his own affairs. His life hadn't been the sort a man bragged about, and he damned well wasn't about to bellyache about the breaks he'd had. So what else was there to talk about?

Besides, it had been his experience that women were more interested in talking about themselves than in hearing some guy's life history, and for once, he was genuinely interested in listening. Hell, he'd even braced himself for another discourse on art.

Instead, she'd sat there looking cool and smooth as a dish of French ice cream and told him all about her grandfather's pigs! Rex was used to letting his mind range freely while a woman rambled on about her personal triumphs, or all the rich, handsome men she swept off her doorstep every morning. From time to time he'd tune back in, massage a little ego and then tune out again. It was the way the game was played—both players knew all the rules, nobody got hurt, and a good time was had by all.

Maybe he was out of practice. Games tend to lose their excitement after a while, and he was no longer a kid.

But he had a feeling this game was different. Not only didn't he know the rules, he was beginning to suspect the stakes might be a little too rich for his blood, as well.

Watching Lu consider a brass cart full of dessert offerings with all the enthusiasm another woman might exhibit for a tray of diamond bracelets or the show window of a fur salon, Rex began silently listing all the reasons why he should get the hell out of town as fast as he could.

While her mountain of whipped-cream-topped, Cointreau-laced chocolate ice cream melted, she propped her elbows on the table and described the way a cow cautioned the fearlessness out of a newborn calf in those first few moments after it was born.

Then, seeing the cherry sliding gently toward the edge of the crystal bowl, she bit her lower lip and scowled. Fascinated, he watched as she maneuvered it onto her spoon and into her mouth, closing her eyes to savor the sweetness.

Holy geez! Rex shifted in his chair. He watched her tongue touch the tip of a spoonful of dark chocolate ice cream as if she'd just had a glimpse beyond the pearly gates. She sighed. He tugged at his collar. Then, gesturing with her spoon, she tried to describe the way a newly cut field felt under bare feet before the dew had dried, and the distinctive taste of fresh sourwood honey, and all he could think of was the textures of her body and the cool, ice-creamy way her lips would taste just now.

Her voice was husky, pitched low enough to be easy on the ears. Her laughter came softly and often, and he deliberately provoked it, drinking in the sound the way a parched earth drank in rain. She was a desirable woman, he told himself—that's all it was. Purely biological. It had simply been too long since he'd had a woman—and a man had certain needs.

But by the time she got around to telling him about the king snake that had gotten trapped in the parlor and crawled up inside the workings of her grandmother's old pump organ, he knew it was a damned sight more than simple biology.

God, we don't stand a snowball's chance, he swore silently. From the cradle on, they'd been headed in different directions.

Unbidden, his mind slipped back some thirty-odd years. He saw a gangling boy of about nine, his hands too large and his clothes too small. He was dragging a tearful toddler into a cluttered backyard where a tired-looking woman was pegging clothes to a line.

"I found him and he was crying, and he ain't got nowhere to go, Miz Scales. Can I keep him?"

"No you can't, John Jones. You just take him on back where you found him and turn him loose. He's probably one of Ina Pritchert's new young'uns. She lost one, and she's been running all over creation looking for him. And before you ask me again, no, you can't have no dog, neither! The county don't pay me to feed no stray dogs.''

"He could have half my food, Miz Scales."

"You eat more'n any three kids I got a'ready, boy. Take that young'un on back now and give him to Ina. You got dishes to wash.''

Rex tightened his mouth, deepening the grooves that scored his weathered cheeks. It had been years since he'd thought of that. He hoped to hell the kid, whoever he was, had fared better than he had. Babies usually got adopted; sullen brats whose mothers didn't want them but who refused to sign them away were another matter. Scared, resentful, distrustful, he hadn't made it easy for any of the poor women who'd taken him in and done their best for him under difficult circumstances.

There'd been no kindly grandparents waiting with outstretched arms to comfort a scared and hurting kid. Earlier today, he'd watched Lu dealing with what she thought were tough kids. They'd made wisecracks about nudes and jammed trash behind frames, and she hadn't turned a hair. Big deal. If she'd known him at about the same age, she'd have taken one look and called the cops on general principles, and he couldn't have blamed her much.

"So after all that, how'd you get involved with a gallery?'' he asked, sliding smoothly back into the present.

"Through Andrew. My husband."

Rex felt his muscles tighten warningly. So far she'd spoken only of her girlhood. Those kinds of memories were one thing. Memories of a lover, a husband, a man she'd once cared for enough to marry—that was another thing altogether.

Rex realized that he was jealous of a dead man and tried to call up a degree of shame. "It was his gallery?"

"It was his dream." Lu told him about Andrew's uphill struggle to introduce art classes to the county schools, about his subsequent appointment to a statewide post and the collection he'd spent years putting together. "He got tired of hearing the same old excuse whenever he tried to promote local arts—that to be good, art had to come from New York or some other big art center. Andrew's theory was that a lot of the New York art is produced by people from Racine or Pascagoula, from Hickory or High Point—even from Culhane County. People who went to New York to make a name for themselves. The New York and Paris galleries might grab most of the headlines in the slick publications, but that's only a small part of the story."

Rex, who didn't give a damn about slick publications or what was produced where, found himself watching her mouth. There was a faint sheen on her lower lip, and he'd have sold his soul for the privilege of licking it off.

"So you see, Andrew's plan—" Lu went on. The hell with Andrew, he thought irreverently "—was to collect the best of the area artists' work so that children could see what was being produced right here in their own home state."

"Looks like he succeeded," Rex said a little sourly. Why couldn't this guy she'd married have sold hard-

ware? When it came to glamorous topics of conversation, power-plant conversion was right up there
alongside hauling trash to the local landfill. This Andrew of hers, with his slick publications and his New
York galleries, had probably been as smooth as Ten-
nessee sippin' whiskey.

"Unfortunately he died before he ever got it together. The works he'd collected were still hung hel-
ter-skelter all over the house, waiting until we could
renovate the front rooms, when Andrew had his heart
attack. A day later, he was . . . gone."

"Oh, God," Rex said softly. All around them people were talking, laughing. A piano was playing softly
in the background, and a waiter was hovering, ready
to pounce at the slightest indication of need. "Let's get
out of here, shall we?"

As soon as they were settled in the plush, custom-
ized van, Rex put on a tape. It was country music,
simple, mellow and poignant. He wasn't ready to talk.
His common sense and his libido were having a hell of
an argument, and he was caught somewhere in the
middle.

Lu tried to relax, but she was far too aware of the
man beside her. Something was bothering him. Was it
because she'd chattered on and on about things he
couldn't possibly be interested in? Probably. It was so
rare that she got to indulge in any adult conversation.
Questions like, "Did you schedule enough computer
time for all the extensions, Tallulah?" and "Do you
have the 1099 file copies done?" never required an es-
say answer.

Even the weekends were little better. She got a lot of young jocks who'd signed up for art in school because it was supposed to be easy. The gallery was part of the curriculum, and they delighted in embarrassing her. She tended to race through the spiel and let the art teachers handle any questions, which might be good politics, but it didn't make for challenging conversation.

She sighed. Okay, so she was starved for good adult conversation. There was no need to take it out on one man. She'd rattled on all evening, not even having the grace to ask about his work, his family and his hometown. Oh, she might have ventured a question or two, but before he could answer, she was off and running with another tale of adventure on the life and times of a small-time farmer! Talk about adult conversation!

No wonder he looked so grim. He probably had an earache. Even as out of practice as she was, Lu knew that the quickest way to interest a man was to get him to talking about himself. So what had she given him? A monologue!

Did she want to interest Rex Jones?

Against her better judgment, against every rational cell in her brain, Lu knew she did. They probably had nothing at all in common; he wasn't even from Culhane County, but from Texas, of all places! Somehow she couldn't see him moving into the rooms above the Andrew C. Lavender Memorial Gallery.

Tallulah Jones, she mused. Mr. and Mrs. Rex—

Oh, for crying out loud! One date and she was printing up wedding announcements. There were other alternatives. This was hardly the dark ages, even if it sometimes felt that way. With a little discretion, a woman could have a perfectly lovely affair with no harm done and no one the wiser.

How would she handle it if he tried to seduce her?

How would she handle it if he *didn't*?

Rex drove with a skill that was automatic, which was a good thing. His mind wasn't on what he was doing. He had a position to reassess, and a helluva lot of new data to assimilate. It had always been his policy never to go into anything unprepared. In this case, he seemed to have overlooked two key factors, the first of which was this Andrew guy.

Any man who could lure a woman like Lu into devoting her whole life to fulfilling his dreams would be a pretty formidable opponent, dead or alive.

Which brought him to the second factor. Rex wanted Lu Lavender. He'd wanted her the first time he'd laid eyes on her, but he'd figured it was the same old kind of wanting he experienced whenever he saw an extraordinarily attractive woman.

He'd been wrong. What he was feeling now was powerful enough to scare the hell out of him. The last time he'd felt anything even faintly like it had been with Kelli—and he'd married her. He'd loved her with all the idealism of a half-baked kid who still thought every problem had a solution if only one worked hard enough to find it.

He'd learned. He'd spent a lifetime learning. Kelli had been only one more lesson among many, but it was during that period when the truth had finally sunk in. There were no solutions, only trade-offs. Kelli hadn't been willing to stick it out, and he'd been too damned proud to beg. He'd let her go and told himself it was better for both of them.

Better, hell! The truth was that at that point, he'd been shell-shocked. He hadn't even known what was happening to him, much less whether they had a future. As it turned out, they hadn't.

And now he had an uncomfortable feeling he was setting himself up for another no-win situation. Ever since his marriage had ended, he'd fared pretty well by staying clear of any involvement that went beyond skin deep. Until now.

The trouble was, this thing had come on too fast to duck. He'd seen her and wanted her and figured, why not give it a try? So he'd dragged out the old line that had worked pretty well for him since he'd come east, only he'd been the one to trip over it. The lady didn't play by the rules. First thing he'd known, he was in over his head, and now he was afraid he wanted more than she would be willing to give.

Or more than he was in any position to take.

The first time he'd seen Lu swinging up the hillside with a stringer of fish and a cane pole, her face all soft and sun flushed, and her hair curling around that silly duckbilled cap, he'd wanted to tumble her right there in the grass and spend a long, lazy afternoon making love to her. He'd been so busy planning his own line of attack that he hadn't stopped to consider all the possibilities.

Then he'd seen her at the post office, and he'd fallen even deeper under her spell. She probably didn't even know what she was doing to him. Women were different from men. Their defenses were different, probably because their vulnerabilities were different. He didn't blame them for looking after themselves—God knows, he hadn't been able to look after Kelli, and as for his mother...

But a woman like Lu Lavender? He wasn't even sure she *had* any defenses. Fourth-generation lady, cane pole, green sneakers and all, she had no business getting mixed up with a rough-edged bum with a background like his, a man who'd once tangled with the law and barely escaped.

Besides, there was this late husband of hers. She kept talking about Andrew this and Andrew that—*his* gallery, *his* pet theories and *his* fancy position. It was bad enough to get involved with a woman like Lu in the first place, much less a woman who couldn't let go of the past.

Rex couldn't handle that. He'd never before realized how possessive he was, but he knew in his heart that if he ever claimed this woman, there'd be no room for barriers between them. No room for ghosts. Not hers—not his.

He pulled up in front of the three-story house, with its gingerbread, its fancy wrought-iron fence and the granite monument in the front yard. He'd already read the words on the bronze plaque, and they hadn't made him feel a damned bit better about the situation he found himself involved in.

"I didn't ask if there was somewhere else you'd like to go," he said, speaking for the first time since they'd headed home.

"Not really." Lu had been engaged in a delicious, if rather embarrassing, daydream. "There aren't many places to go in a town like Parrish Falls. Most people go out to supper on Friday or Saturday night, and of course, there's church, but that's about it.''

''There's fishing,'' he reminded her, making a deliberate effort to shake off his somber mood.

''There's fishing,'' she agreed with a smile. ''I hate to admit it, but I usually skip church to go out to the pond. I only get two half days off a week, and the thought of having to dress up and play lady on a Sunday morning is just too much.''

Rex smiled, too. Now that he'd brought her home, 'he found he wasn't ready for the evening to end. Still, he couldn't afford to rush into anything, not until he was damned sure of what he was doing. One step at a time, he promised himself, and tonight's step had better not take him inside her house. The practical side of him might caution against moving too fast, but he'd been known to go against its best advice in the past.

''I enjoyed dinner a lot, Rex. Thank you for asking me.''

They strolled up to the front porch, and he studied the way the yellow light from the ornate fixture over the door struck her hair, haloing each strand. The cream was gone from her lips. Evidently she'd chewed it off on the drive home. He'd like to have chewed it off for her. And spread some more and licked that off, and spread some more . . .

He shifted uncomfortably and cleared his throat. Never had he felt like such a clumsy ox! She came up to the top button of his shirt, and he could easily have hefted her in one arm. She was a lady in the very best sense of the word, and he'd had damned little experience with ladies in his life. "Yeah, well—like I said, I was alone, and I don't know many people in town…"

Lu felt disappointment rise like bitter medicine in her throat. Was that it? He'd only asked her because he was truly tired of his own company? She'd thought—that is, she'd hoped…

"I guess I'd better say good-night. It's getting late. My goodness, it's almost ten o'clock," she said brightly.

Fumbling at the lock, she managed to get the key in the keyhole, yanking the knob and twisting it at the same time. "All this humidity," she mumbled when he continued to hover over her shoulder. "Everything swells up." Why didn't he just leave? Did that Texas chivalry he turned on and off like a light switch demand that he do his duty and actually see her safely through her door? Dammit, she didn't *want* to be a duty—she wanted to be a pleasure!

"Lu, promise me you'll have dinner with me again tomorrow night?"

"What?" She turned slowly, and he was closer than she'd expected. To keep her balance, she almost grabbed his belt, stopping herself just in time. Instead, she flattened her heated palms on the cool surface of the door behind her.

"Just promise me," he said urgently. "Do it—please, Lu?"

"Well, all right, if it means so much to you, but this time, I—"

He didn't give her a chance to finish. He slipped his arms around her even as he bent down, and before she could utter a sound, his mouth absorbed her startled protest.

Never had anything seemed so wonderfully, achingly right! Lu thought her entire life had been leading up to this moment as Rex's arms tightened, holding her against a body that felt like warm granite. Warm, living granite!

Heat lightning flickered off to the west. It seemed a perfectly natural consequence of his mouth on hers, of his hands tangling in her hair, sliding slowly down her back to cup the shape of her hips. His tongue probed between her lips, seeking entrance. How could something feel so hard and so soft at the same time?

Deep inside her, fires that had once burned with a cozy, comfortable warmth now threatened to blaze out of control. Lu found herself clinging to those massive shoulders for safety as he fanned the flames still higher. He dragged his lips away, breathing heavily. She could feel the thunder of his heart moving his whole body, as if he were an elemental part of the storm that flickered over the mountains surrounding their narrow valley.

A rock slide of a man. Hadn't she thought of him in those very terms the first time she'd laid eyes on him? For all the gentleness she sensed deep inside him, physically he was all sharp angles and rugged planes, hard as bedrock and every bit as unyielding.

Still clinging, she shuddered, and he pressed her face against his chest. In an effort to minimize the difference in their heights, he'd spread his legs apart and assumed a slouching stance instead of his usual erect bearing. As far as Lu was concerned, it was disastrous! He was taut as a bowstring, and she was in the same condition. She was afraid to move a muscle for fear of triggering something she wasn't ready for. They were practically strangers. This was their first date! She was supposed to be an experienced woman, and she hadn't the slightest idea how all this had happened.

It was Rex who finally took control. With hands that were strong, if trembling, he clasped her arms, steadying her as he stepped back. Lu thought she heard him drawl a soft oath, but with the thunder and two sets of lungs gasping for air, she couldn't be sure.

The way her head was reeling, she couldn't be sure of her own name!

"I'm right sorry about that, ma'am. Like you said, it must be all this humidity. Something must have shorted out."

Lu hiccupped. She closed her eyes and prayed to be granted invisibility. When that didn't happen, she opened them again, sighed, and said, "Yes, well . . . I expect I'd better get inside before the storm breaks. Rex, thank you." *Hiccup!* "For dinner, I mean. I'll probably be seeing you again before you leave."

"You're damned right you will, ma'am—pardon my profanity. You promised to have dinner with me tomorrow night, and if there's one thing I'll lay odds on, it's that Miz Lavender's a woman of her word."

That Texas blarney again. "When the going gets tough, the tough play cowboy, right?" she said, laughing shakily.

"Or hiccup."

"A gentleman would pretend not to notice."

"Notice what, Miz Lavender? I didn't notice a single, solitary thing, ma'am."

He chuckled, and she joined in, grateful for any means of relieving the tension. "You're spreading it on again, Mr. Jones. The minute I hear a 'ma'am' out of you, I can't help but wonder what you're up to."

"I can't help but wonder, too, Lu," he said softly, catching her chin and tilting it so that the light fell on her face. "When I find out, I promise you'll be the first to know."

With that, he kissed her again, hard and much too quickly. Lu was sagging against the doorframe when he leaped down the steps and practically ran out to the van.

The phone was ringing when she let herself inside, but she wasn't in time to catch it. It would probably be Mrs. Potts next door, with a not-so-subtle hint about respectability and the behavior expected of a woman of her standing in the community.

There was an unusual glow about her, Lu had to admit. Standing before the bathroom mirror, she studied herself closely, something she hadn't bothered to do in ages. From her mother she'd inherited the sort of skin that seemed a gift from the gods at age twenty—no pores, no blemishes, good color with little need for makeup.

By the time she'd reached thirty, she'd realized that it was also the type of skin that demanded a lot of care to prevent the formation of wrinkles. Lu had enough patience to apply sunscreen and moisturizer, but that was about the extent of it. At thirty-seven she figured she was due a few fine lines around her eyes and a few silver strands among the black ones.

It had never bothered her before, but then Andrew had been eighteen years older than she. She'd wanted to look more mature, though he'd always looked young for his age. He'd been lean and fit, burning up energy with the intensity of his personality rather than with physical exercise. He'd been an ambitious man, dedicated to his own ideals, and she'd loved him dearly, even during the times when he'd treated her as he might a favorite niece, irritated by the gaps in her education.

Andrew had studied and painted in New York for several years before they'd met. He'd been in Raleigh for an exhibit of his work one fall, and she'd attended the opening, not because she was interested in art, but because they were from the same area.

He'd told her she had the rustic charm of a milk-maid and the most flawless bone structure he'd ever seen and asked her to sit for him. She'd been flattered but too timid to take him up on it. Before she quite knew how it came about, she'd been neatly swept off her feet.

Her farm background hadn't seemed to bother him at first, though there'd been times during the eleven years of their marriage when she'd felt as if he were being slightly condescending. Nevertheless, she'd read the books he'd recommended and trekked after him from museum to museum, even on their honeymoon, listening as he explained what was good and what was bad and why. He'd been a good husband, and she'd never had cause to doubt his faithfulness. She prided herself that theirs had been a relationship based on mutual respect as well as love.

But it had all been so long ago. She'd been living alone for six years now, dating on rare occasions, but without the slightest effect on her emotions. And then, along came a man as different from Andrew as night from day, and before she could even catch her breath, ashes she'd thought had long since burned out had caught fire again and were blazing up higher than ever before.

Placing a hand on each side of her face, Lu lifted and pulled back. A face lift? Maybe a new dress. Dear heavens, certainly some new lingerie! She'd worn her wedding things until the elastic had died, and then re- placed them with utilitarian white cotton from the Sears catalog.

Not that there was any reason to get all hot and bothered about such a thing as new underwear at this point. All right, so she still had a few viable hor- mones in her body—there was no way she could con- duct an affair in this town without it being common knowledge, no matter how much she might will it otherwise.

By now, the phone lines were probably burning up with a blow-by-blow description of that kiss.

A throb-by-throb description would be more like it. Dear Lord, what a man! What an unlikely thing to happen to her, here in her own hometown, of all places. On the rare occasions when she'd even thought about the possibility of meeting another man, she'd taken it for granted she'd have to leave home first. She knew everyone in Parrish Falls, and there were defi- nitely no contenders. The eligible bachelors old enough to shave consisted of poor old Hector and Ira

Tate down at the Farmer's Exchange, and somehow she couldn't see herself ever being quite that desperate.

While she was searching for pluckable white hairs, the phone rang again. It could be Rex, wanting to say good-night. Come to think of it, they'd never gotten around to wishing each other good-night. At least not officially.

Breathlessly she snatched up the receiver, her eyes sparkling in anticipation.

"Tallulah, are you all right?"

She wasn't. She felt as if she'd been sandbagged. "Oh. Hector. Well, sure I'm all right—why wouldn't I be?"

"I don't have to tell you, my dear, that a woman in your position can't be too careful. I was out taking my evening constitutional and I just happened to see a suspicious-looking van parked out in front of your house, half hidden by that big poplar. Now I know you're a kind-hearted woman, Tallulah, and you'd be the last person in the world to suspect someone just because he happened to be a stranger with no visible means of support, but—"

"Hector, did you call me up at this time of night just to nag me about something that's none of your business?"

"Now, now, let's not get upset, shall we? I only wanted to inform you that a certain strange man, the same one who was hanging around the gallery earlier today, has been asking questions all over town about you. Clarence Timmons told me he's been seen out at that motel near the interstate, and you know what sort of people a place like that attracts.''

"It happens to be the only motel within twenty miles," Lu snapped. She was thoroughly fed up with this sanctimonious old buzzard poking his nose into her business. It was bad enough when he wanted to tell her how to run the gallery, but when he started trying to choose her friends for her, that was going too far! "Hector, I'm certainly old enough to look after myself. I've been doing it for a good many years now. You're perfectly welcome to visit the gallery anytime you please during open hours, but once it closes, I'd appreciate it if you'd respect my privacy." Which was as near as she could bring herself to telling him to mind his own business.

She hung up on his sputtering protestations, feeling angry, resentful and frustrated. How dared he spoil things for her! He didn't know Rex, and she did. How *dared* he presume to judge a man when he didn't know the first thing about him?

And just how much do you know about him, Tallulah?

Okay—not all that much. He came from Texas, but so did a lot of other people. He had a logo on the side of his van, but if he'd deliberately designed it to be difficult to read, he couldn't have done a better job. Did that mean he was a shady character?

Angrily she picked up her yellow-and-white print dress and slung it against a bentwood rocker, where it slithered to the floor. Damn polyester. Damn rocking chairs!

Damn all foolish, middle-aged dreamers who take one look at a stranger named Jones and start making out wedding invitation lists! She'd been getting along just fine before he'd come riding into town with his Texas blarney and charmed his way right into her heart.

Her heart?

"Oh, don't be stupid, Tallulah. You're certainly old enough to know the difference between love and lust."

Four

Lu awoke reluctantly six days a week. She was never particularly eager to begin another day of typing and filing, or staying inside to conduct visitors through the gallery when she would much rather have been outside doing almost anything else.

Sundays were different. Whether she planned a trip to the farm, a drive along the Blue Ridge Parkway or nothing more than a lazy morning in the backyard hammock reading the latest paperback thriller and pulling the occasional weed from among the overgrown shrubbery, she invariably bounded out of bed before the sun cleared the horizon on Sunday mornings.

On a day like today, when sweltering heat inevitably trailed a mere hour or two behind the sun, she liked to take her first cup of coffee out into the backyard while the grass was still damp with dew. It was too shady for much of a vegetable garden, and she didn't dare do too much to the shrubs that had probably been planted by some noteworthy Lavender ancestor in the Year One, but at least she could enjoy the relative privacy to be found at that time of morning behind all the overgrown hedges and overhanging trees. To peer into her backyard from the house next door, Lana Potts would have to drag the kitchen table over to the window. Lu seriously doubted if even Lana would go that far.

The coffee was still dripping when the door buzzer sounded. Adrenaline raced through her body. *No* one came to call at six-thirty in the morning, not even the nosiest of neighbors. Late-night phone calls and early-morning callers usually meant only one thing—trouble. Either someone was sick or her street was going to be blocked off for roadwork or the office had burned down last night.

She had only one relative left—her second cousin Ralph, who ran a sawmill over in Surry County. Ralph must have had an accident. How many times had she warned him about using that old makeshift equipment? Hurrying to the front door, Lu flung it wide.

The *last* thing she expected to see was Rex Jones, his hair damp and slicked back, a watermelon-wide grin on his craggy face and a wicker basket in his hand. "Morning, Miz Lavender, ma'am. I saw your kitchen light go on and thought you might like to take your breakfast out on the pond with me. Going to be a real scorcher today—too hot to be heatin' up the house with cooking."

Joy streaked through her like the clear triumphant notes of a trumpet, and she clutched the doorframe. "Dammit, Rex, you scared the wits out of me!"

His face fell so quickly that she immediately felt guilty. "Lu, I'm sorry."

What on earth was wrong with her? She hadn't felt this giddy over her first grown-up kiss! Managing with some difficulty to keep a rein on her crazy emotions, she injected a note of sternness into her voice. "You're out of your mind, do you know that? Do you have any idea what time it is?"

His look of guilt gave way to something a little more hopeful, and she groaned. No man as big and tough as Rex Jones had any right looking so...so damned *wistful*! "Oh, all right, as long as you're here, you might as well come on inside," she said grudgingly.

He hung back, his hands looking enormous on the delicate handle of the wicker basket. "I reckon I'm sort of early, huh? I parked out under that big tree so I wouldn't be so conspicuous and waited until I saw your light come on. I've been up for hours. You did say you always went out to the pond on Sunday mornings, didn't you?"

"What I do on Sundays or any other day has nothing to do with it, Rex. The point is, people just don't come calling at this hour of the day. At least not around here. It's...it's just not *done*."

His face fell again, and Lu had to restrain herself forcibly from grabbing him by the arm and dragging him inside. If only he'd waited until a respectable hour...

If only her brain would start functioning!

If only she'd had time to get dressed in something decent instead of this faded old cotton housecoat she'd practically pinned together because it wasn't worth mending. It had blotted the dew off her wrought-iron furniture so many times that the seat was permanently stained. She was barefoot, her hair was uncombed, and any minute now, Mr. Cahill would be passing by on his first lap around the block. He did three before breakfast and three after supper, and he wasn't known for his reticence. By the last lap, everyone in town would know that Lu Lavender had been entertaining a man in her housecoat before the sun was even awake.

That is, if they didn't think she was seeing him off after a night of unbridled passion. "Get in here," she ordered, grabbing him by the arm and practically yanking him through the door. "Are you absolutely bound and determined to ruin my reputation? If so, you're certainly going about it the right way."

Rex stood awkwardly in the tiny foyer that served the gallery, gripping the covered basket in both hands. He looked concerned, embarrassed and utterly loveable, and Lu felt her anger begin to crumble. If she were honest, she would have to admit that she wasn't really angry with him at all. It was sheer defensiveness, a means of keeping her from having to admit just how glad she was to see him.

"Lu, I'm awful sorry. I didn't stop to think how it might look. All I could think about last night on my way out to the Peacock was now nice it would be to catch our breakfast and cook it over an open fire and maybe take a dip later on when the sun got too hot."

His eyes took on an added glint. "Well, maybe not *all* I could think of. I guess I should have asked first, huh?"

"At the very least." How could he do it to her? She was grinning like a jack-o-lantern when by rights she should have been furious with him. "I really ought to send you packing for showing up before I've even had time to get decent, but... Oh, well, as long as you're already here, I suppose it doesn't make that much difference."

"Then you'll have breakfast with me?" His hair was drying even as they stood talking, fast losing any semblance of grooming. Lu had to clench her fists to keep from reaching out and brushing it away from his forehead.

"I was planning to go out to the pond after breakfast. I suppose we might as well go on out now."

A short while later, they were munching doughnuts and watching dragonflies hover over the still, dark water. Rex had allowed her two of the sticky confections and no more, claiming it would spoil her early lunch.

"Optimistic, aren't you?" Lu teased. In her newest old jeans and her best yellow T-shirt, she was lying on her back, legs crossed at the ankle, with her favorite cane pole braced between her toes. She'd dug her own worms and had caught four nice bluegills while Rex, fishing with grasshoppers and an old spinning rod she'd found in the garage, had yet to catch a single fish.

"If I'd taken time to get some decent tackle, it would've been different," he muttered. "I never did cotton much to fish that ate bugs."

Her mind followed a convoluted trail from live bait to licenses to logos on the side of a van. "What does your truck door say? It's so small I can't even read it."

"Shows what I know about advertising, doesn't it? I designed my own logo. Actually I thought it turned out pretty good, but the guy who did the paint job for me didn't seem all that impressed."

"Rex, purely as a matter of interest, what do you have against answering a simple question? Is it a matter of principle, or are you trying to hide a deep, dark past as an international spy?"

Rex lunged for a fat grasshopper and missed. "Maybe I'm just trying to hide a past that's so dull it would bore you stiff," he replied. "Ever think of that?"

She shot him a skeptical look, which he ignored.

The truth was that Rex had learned to keep his own counsel a long time ago. Nothing had happened to him since that had given him any reason to change. Until now. Like it or not, he admitted to himself, if he hoped to get anywhere with a woman like Lu Lavender, he was probably going to have to learn to be more open. He thought that ought to be about as comfortable as having a few wisdom teeth extracted.

Lu shifted impatiently. "Forget I asked."

"No, I was just thinking, that's all. So... what do you want to know?"

Lu shot him a quick look to see if he was serious. What did she want to know? So much she didn't know where to start, that was all. She'd have to go easy on him unless she wanted to scare him away. "I take it the JRJ stands for something Rex Jones, but what's all that fine print down underneath?"

"Engineering consultant. Power plant conversion specialist. Phone number. Mailing address. Satisfied?" He yanked in his line, scowled at the waterlogged bait, and flung it out once more.

"Get much business that way?" she taunted. Through a skein of dark thick lashes, she was having a field day watching the play of sun on the muscles of his deeply tanned torso. As the heat had grown more intense, Rex had taken off his shirt, revealing a back that was even broader than she'd suspected and a chest that was patterned with dark brown hair.

She'd been right about his wearing a low-slung gun belt. His tooled leather belt had settled around a section of his lean hips that was a good five inches below the subtle indentation of his waist.

"Where'd you get those worms you're using, anyway?" he muttered.

With a sigh of surrender, Lu waved a hand in the direction of the pasture. "You go up to the top of the hill, crawl through the barbed wire—don't touch the top strand; it's electric—and flip over the dried patties with a stick. You can usually dig up some fat ones that are busy tilling the soil. That's what earthworms were put on earth to do, you know. Composting. It's their mission in life."

"And then what, you wait until I'm up to my elbows in it and come running up the hill yelling April fool?"

She rolled over onto her side and propped her head in her hand. The fishing had slowed up after the early-morning frenzy. Laying her pole aside, she studied him curiously. "Boy, you sure are suspicious. Didn't you ever go fishing when you were a little boy, Rex?"

"Maybe I never was a little boy."

"A big little boy, then. You certainly didn't pop into this world weighing any two hundred pounds."

"Two-twelve, actually."

Laughter danced in Lu's eyes. "Then or now?"

He ignored her teasing. "What am I supposed to dig with?"

Her gaze moved down to his hands. They were beautiful hands for a man. Andrew's had been soft and smooth, the fingers tapered. Rex's were square-palmed, with long, blunt-tipped fingers and neatly trimmed nails.

An unexpected feeling of breathlessness overcame her, and she sat up. Wiping her hands on her hips, she handed him a plastic container. "Here, try one of mine. No point in digging more if the fish have stopped biting. Tell me about your company, Rex, since I can't read your truck door from here. What does the first J stand for? Is your headquarters in Galveston? Do you travel a lot? Oh—of course! That's what you were doing here that first day I saw you, wasn't it? Davis Power Plant."

Rex retrieved his hook, now bare, and laid his pole aside. If the fish weren't biting, there was no point in sacrificing another tiller of the soil. The truth was, he'd never done all that much fishing—never had the time. His main reason for doing it now was to keep her here so that he could get to know her better and figure out what it was about her that set her apart from all the other women he'd ever met.

For starters, he'd sure as hell never tried to court another woman over a pair of fishing poles in between discussing the finer points of cow patties!

"Okay, you win." He sighed heavily. "It's eighteen months old, John, no, yes, and yes—Davis Power Plant." His expression dared her to ask for more than that.

Lu closed her mouth when it occurred to her that it was hanging slightly open. She was nowhere near ready to concede defeat, but even she knew when a strategic retreat was in order. "Careful there, pa'tner, that might be classified information you're handing out."

His smile was as easy as ever, but there was a certain hardness in his eyes that hadn't been there before. "Not satisfied? Okay, tell me then, Lu—what do you consider the most important data about the men you go out with? Family background? Schools? Clubs? Income? Investment portfolio? Politics?"

It was a moment before she replied, and when she spoke, her voice was subdued. "Was I really all that bad? I'm sorry, Rex. I was interested, that's all. You're not exactly the sort of man I meet every day, and I was—well . . . *interested*."

Guilt set in as he watched her begin to close up like one of those flowers that folds its petals the moment it feels the touch of a human hand. The guilt was followed by defensiveness. Dammit, why should he feel guilty? She'd brought it on herself. She was the one who'd been asking all the questions, not the other way around. Had he asked her who she'd voted for in the last election or whether or not her tetanus booster was up to date?

"Lu, I'm sorry. I guess one of the things I'm trying to hide is a rotten, suspicious disposition."

At his genuine contrition, her petals began to unfold once more. "That's okay. It comes of living alone, no doubt. Actually it's sort of funny, you know—women who live alone get handed all sorts of free advice. Things like how to protect everything from their virtue to their investments, how to change tires and make the house look lived-in when nobody's there. How to prepare for the future—as if anyone could ever really prepare. It never occurred to me that men might get the same sort of advice from well-meaning friends."

"I can't say I've ever been given much advice on changing tires or protecting my virtue," Rex confessed, his face relaxing in a smile. "Plain truth is, I reckon I was born closemouthed and never learned to open up. There's only one thing you need to know about me, Lu. No matter what, I'll never hurt you in any way. I'd cut off my right arm first."

The gravity of his words seemed ill suited for a day when summer droned lazily over every heavy seed-head while autumn whispered through the tops of pink-tinged trees. As if embarrassed by his own emotion, Rex sat up suddenly. "Say, I'm getting hungry again, lady, what about you? We've got two apiece. Think that'll be enough?"

With something like relief, Lu picked up the cue. "Depends on how you feel about a fair division of labor. I caught 'em—you cook 'em."

Rex reached over and brushed a stem of dried grass from her hair, and she trembled at his touch. It was as if he'd somehow touched far more than her hair. It was as if they were connected on some deep, internal level. He had only to look her way and she could actually feel it.

She sat up and flexed her back, pretending she wasn't aware of his nearness with every cell in her body. "That leaves fish-cleaning and fire-building. What about it? I can do either, but I refuse to do both."

"Same here."

"No choices? Good. I hate to dress fish. Although if you're no better at dressing fish than you are at catching them, maybe you'd better see if you can start a fire."

"Hey, go easy on the put-downs, will you? I'm a real pain when my ego gets trampled underfoot," Rex countered gently.

"Oops—sorry. *Can* you build a fire?" As if she didn't know. As if he hadn't already struck enough sparks to set a forest ablaze.

"Yep."

"Were you ever a Boy Scout?"

"Nope."

"Can I trust you not to set the woods on fire?"

"Yep."

Torn between amusement and exasperation, Lu sighed heavily. "Jones, what is it with you and simple conversation? Does talking bore you? Do *I* bore you? Is there a code of silence among you Texas he-men that I don't know about?'' Snatching up her pole, she yanked it out of the water, and a tiny bream flew over her head. Groaning, she scrambled to her feet. "Oh, Lord, I've killed him now. I didn't even know he was there.''

Chasing the flapping fish through the ankle-high grass, she finally caught him in her hands and slipped the small hook from his mouth before easing him back into the pond. "There, you poor baby, go back and find your mama.''

"Think he'll make it?'' Rex, still sitting on the bank with his arms wrapped around his knees, had watched the whole exercise.

"For today, at least. Sooner or later they all get caught, if not by a fisherman, by a snapping turtle, and if not by a turtle, by a bigger fish. Sort of sad, isn't it?''

"Another one of life's little trade-offs. The perfect solution for hungry fish and fishermen doesn't set too well with little guys like that who end up being someone's dinner.''

Lu's face fell. "I could have gone a long time without thinking about that. So maybe I won't go fishing for a while.'' She rinsed her fingers at the edge of the water and sank back on the crushed grass. "Want to change the subject before we start lunch? Weren't you about to tell me all about your nonfishing childhood and your Texas engineering outfit, and how on earth you came to be here in Parrish Falls and how long you plan on staying?''

Particularly the latter, she added silently. It was growing more and more imperative that she know how long he would be around.

In one easy motion, Rex got to his feet. As he stood over her, his face in shadow, a shaft of late-morning sunlight slanted through the locust trees to etch a golden rim around his head and shoulders. Lu thought it was one of the most beautiful sights she'd ever seen, right up there with rime ice on Mount Mitchell and a laurel slick in the springtime.

"Richmond, not Texas," Rex said gently. "I'll tell you the rest of the stuff while the fish are cooking—not that there's anything to tell. Say, are you sure the owner of this place doesn't mind if we build a fire?"

"Richmond, not Texas. Wow! I really hit a gusher that time, didn't I?" But her words were teasing, the smile in her eyes far warmer than she knew. "Gus doesn't mind, Rex. See that circle of rocks up under that tree on the hill? I used to build fires there as a little girl."

"And as a big one, if I remember correctly," he reminded her with a slow grin. "Marshmallows in the rain?"

"They're a mess," she confessed. Reaching out a hand, she allowed herself to be pulled to her feet. "The ants always managed to get in the bag before I could close it up again, and they're impossible to get out without dumping the whole bag, and that only attracts more."

"Another one of life's little trade-offs. Ants don't eat a whole lot, but of course, if you begrudge a hardworking ant his daily sugar fix..."

Lu watched in fascination as one corner of his lips twitched, then lifted, and then his white teeth were flashing at her, chipped front corner and all, and she was lost again.

"Are we really talking about ants and marshmallows?" she asked wonderingly. "I think I'm in over my head, Rex. Either I've forgotten all the rules, or you don't play fair."

"Honey, did it ever occur to you that maybe I'm not playing?"

She moaned softly. Afterwards she didn't know whether she leaned forward or he reached out and gathered her close, but suddenly nothing else mattered. Fish, ants and marshmallows were all forgotten. Texas or Richmond, it made no difference—there were no questions so urgent that they couldn't wait. He clasped her face in his hands and smiled down at her, and she could see the green depths of his eyes, the golden rims, the tangle of lashes. Finally she shut her own in sheer self-defense.

Sanity kicked one last time as it struggled to reach the surface. "Rex...?" she whispered just before he brought his mouth down on hers. And then it was too late.

Imprisoned against his sun-warm body, impressed by every hard contour, she felt the world tilt, felt the very foundation of her safe, sane existence threatened. His heart was pounding, but no more than hers. She could feel the fine tremor of his hands as he tangled them in her hair and then moved restlessly down her back.

He tasted of coffee and a minty sweetness that was all his own, as his tongue explored and caressed. His hands moved restlessly over her back, curving over her hips and moving upward again to touch the delicate bones of her shoulder. Inside she was melting, and the heat had nothing at all to do with with the August sun.

"Oh, God, I could lay you down in the grass and take you right here, and it still wouldn't be enough," Rex vowed roughly, his ragged breath bringing chills to the damp skin of her throat.

"Oh, yes . . . please!"

Had she actually said that? She felt feverish, not herself at all. The only reality was the two of them and what was happening between them. Nothing else mattered.

Rex hung on to his control by a shred, wishing he dared let go. He slipped one hand between them with some dim idea of putting space between their straining bodies, but when he encountered the firm swell of her breast, he groaned aloud. Unable to stop himself, he turned his hand until his palm cupped the sweet mound, staring down to see his own dark, callused hand caressing the soft, yellow-clad shape. Mesmerized, he watched as his thumb brushed back and forth over the peak that was clearly defined under the knit material.

He'd never wanted anything so much in all his life. He hadn't brought her out here to make love to her, at least not consciously. And not in broad daylight, beside a public road. It was just that when he touched her, when he even thought about touching her this way, he started falling apart.

It had never happened to him before, not like this. He wished to hell it hadn't happened now, not with someone like Lu Lavender. She wasn't the type of woman a man could enjoy for a while and then walk away from, not even if he wanted to.

The trouble was, he was afraid he wouldn't even want to walk away. And that was what terrified him.

He slid his hand away from her breast and pressed her against him, lowering his face to the top of her head so that he wouldn't have to look her in the eyes. He couldn't face those eyes of hers, not yet. Not unless he was ready to surrender his very soul. It was tough enough just holding her this way, with her hair like silk under his cheek and the fresh scent of her eddying up on currents of body heat, like a field of bluebonnets after a rain.

He needed more time. He needed to think, dammit, and she wasn't making it any easier for him! Remember all those lessons you learned in the past, man—the trade-offs, the problems that just don't have any solutions! Don't ruin your life again.

He tried to tell himself that Lu Lavender was just another small-town woman—decent, attractive and available. He'd always had an easy way with women. They liked him, and he liked them; it was just that simple. He'd always taken what he needed from them and given generously in return, and as far as he knew, not one of them had ever had cause to complain.

But he always had sense enough to stick to women who wouldn't get hurt, who wouldn't ask for more than he had to give. And he'd learned to put a lid on his own expectations. No shooting for the limit. In order to survive, a man had to set his sights on realistic goals.

He hadn't quite mastered that one at eighteen; even so, his marriage to Kelli had seemed realistic at the time. She'd come up pretty much the way he had, making her own way from the time she was sixteen. They should have been able to make it. The odds had been with them.

For a while after the trouble in Galveston, he'd been too bitter for even the most basic relationship, but that hadn't lasted, thank God. With Kelli gone, he'd needed a woman. He'd needed a lot of things—anything to keep him from lying awake nights thinking of what had happened, letting it eat into him and corrode his soul.

He'd gotten straightened out again, but it had taken a few years. Years when he'd just skimmed the surface, filling the days with bone-breaking work and the nights with whatever the nights had offered. He'd grown tired of calling women ''honey'' because he couldn't remember their names. He'd settled for the work.

And the work had been enough. That is, it had until a few days ago, when he'd seen a woman who had knocked him six ways to Sunday! He'd wiped his sweaty palms on the seat of his jeans and started trying to recall the little he'd ever learned about how a gentleman was supposed to treat a lady.

And now he was holding her in his arms with his heart going like a five-alarm fire, and his whole life was flashing past his eyes!

Lu began to pull away, and reluctantly he eased his hold, not quite freeing her. She tugged down her T-shirt. "Would you mind giving me breathing room?" she demanded tightly.

Oh, hell! He tried to protect her from his own worst intentions, and she thought he was rejecting her. "Lu, sweetheart, please try to understand. For once in my life I'm trying to do the responsible thing. I told you I'd never do anything to hurt you."

So much for gallantry. Although, at the moment Rex wasn't sure which one of them he was trying to protect—her or himself.

She lifted her head and stared at him coolly, her lips still warm from his kisses. "You and your damned white hat. What makes you think you know what's best for me?"

"Lu, be sensible," he pleaded.

"Maybe I don't want to be sensible." Maybe she wanted him to sweep her off her feet and make wild, passionate love to her so that she wouldn't have to bear the responsibility for her own actions. Afterward, after he'd gone, she could comfort herself with the knowledge that she hadn't been given time to consider whether she really wanted a temporary affair with a perfect stranger. "All right, so it was an irresponsible impulse," she conceded grudgingly. "Now and then—at least every dozen or so years—I've been known to harbor an irresponsible notion."

"Yeah, I can see you now, ripping tags off pillows right and left and tromping all around the Keep Off the Grass signs. This is a little different, honey. Besides, it's hardly the place to start something. What would your neighbors think?''

"Oh, stop shoving my neighbors down my throat," she grumbled, backing away and smoothing her hair with unsteady hands. "I know you're right, I just don't particularly enjoy being turned on and off like a faucet."

"Lu, I didn't deliberately plan what happened. Okay, so maybe I might've *thought* about it a few times. About what it would be like, I mean—hell, we both know there's something between us. I just figured we'd better back off and take another look before we get in over our heads."

He was right, of course. If she'd been the one to break it up, she'd be feeling all smug and self-righteous. Instead she was feeling just plain frustrated!

Rex ventured a smile. Unfortunately it was one of those crinkly, chip-toothed ones that she invariably found impossible to resist. "You're a real menace, Rex Jones. There ought to be warnings posted whenever you cross a state line."

"Honey, you were never in any real danger."

"*Now* you tell me," she said witheringly, and he laughed aloud.

"Keep on, why don't you? You're playing with some pretty high voltage."

"Ooooh?" she drawled.

His eyes glinted. "Y'know something? Nice ladies can be a real pain. As a rule, I light outta town the minute one comes sniffin' around, but you just keep on pushing, honey—I can make you the exception."

"Are you calling me a nice lady?" Lu planted her fists on her hips.

"Yeah, I'm calling you a nice lady," he growled softly. "And I've just discovered that I've got a re-eal mean sweet tooth for nice ladies."

"Well, then?" she taunted him, only half joking.

"I've done a lot of wicked things in my life, ma'am, but rolling a nice lady in the hay on a Sunday morning in plain view of the whole town isn't one of them."

"How very noble of you. Isn't there a medal for that sort of thing? The noble prize?"

"Lu . . ." he said warningly. "You're pushing it."

"Maybe this nice lady feels like living dangerously for a change. For six years I've lived like a goldfish in a small bowl. Actually all my life. I don't know how things are in Galveston or Richmond or wherever, but in Parrish Falls, you know everybody, everybody knows you, and a woman in my position is considered a . . . a sort of civic responsibility. One of these days I'm going to be summoned to the courthouse and told that they've just appointed a Lu Lavender committee to come up with a ten-year plan for my future."

The smile had faded from Rex's face, and he looked genuinely concerned. Lu wished she'd had the good sense to shut up before she'd ever opened her mouth. "Sorry," she said with a whimsical smile. "It's called the goldfish bowl syndrome—it'll pass. It's usually worse when the days start getting shorter. Put it down to biorhythms or photosynthesis—one of those natural phenomena the health magazines are full of."

He could put it down to boredom. He could put it down to anything except the truth—that she was dangerously infatuated with a man she hardly even knew.

"Let's put it down to hunger, hmm?" Rex wrapped an arm around her waist and turned her toward the locust grove, where they'd left the charcoal and a small stack of kindling. He was being kind and tactful, and that was even more embarrassing, Lu thought miserably.

"Yes—I'm starving." With a twist, she freed herself and moved out in front of him, but he caught up with her easily, tugging her back into his arms.

"*You're* starving! I've never been so hungry in my life," he said gruffly, burying his face in her sun-warmed hair.

Half-heartedly, she tried to disengage herself once more. She lacked the strength—too weak from hunger, no doubt. "Rex, don't start again."

"Honey, I can't seem to help myself. I thought if we ignored it, it would go away, but it only gets worse."

"Try harder."

"Sorry. I've already given it my best shot."

Lu could feel herself sinking fast. "Maybe if we talked about it . . ."

"You're really hung up on words, aren't you? Is that something all you nice ladies have in common?"

"I'm only trying to help."

"Okay, so we'll talk it out. How about if I tell you that what I'd like to do first of all is to lift your shirt over your head and let the sun shine down on your breasts? Then I'd like to—"

Lu moaned softly and leaned her forehead against his chest. "Stop it," she moaned.

"Honey, I wish I could. Somehow, I don't think talking's going to help much."

"I know. I don't want to talk, either, but—Rex, it's just too soon to be feeling this way. I'm not handling things at all gracefully, but I honestly don't think I'm going to get much better with time."

"What do you say we give it a try, all the same? Maybe if we get to know each better you'll feel more comfortable."

"Comfortable?" She sighed. Her gaze fell to the front of her soft T-shirt, where two small bumps pushed proudly at the fabric. Doubt began to mingle with frustrated desire and embarrassment. Had she magnified this whole thing into more than it really was? A kiss or two—a simple pass; it wasn't as if he'd asked her to marry him, for goodness' sake. Now that she considered it, he was acting rather strangely, too— as if he'd unleashed a tiger and didn't know quite how to get it back in the cage.

As if sensing her doubts, Rex smoothed her hair back from her face to look down into her eyes. "Lu, no woman's ever had this effect on me before. To tell you the truth, it makes me nervous. You sort of knocked me off my pins the first time I ever laid eyes on you, and the feeling's grown stronger ever since."

"You were the one who stopped things just now."

Rex blew a stream of air toward his brow, stirring the unruly hair that had fallen forward. "Whew! You don't pull your punches, do you?" The glint in his eyes said he was teasing, but there was a ragged edge of tension in his voice, the drawl scarcely noticeable.

"Not about things that matter."

"And this matters to you?"

Lu nodded mutely. Just why it mattered so deeply, she wasn't sure; she only knew it did. Rex mattered to her.

"There's a lot you don't know about me, Lu."

She let out a breath with a husky laugh. "Tell me about it! Don't you think I haven't noticed that under all that folksy down-home charm of yours, you don't let slip a single drop of real information?"

"I told you how much I weighed." His smile was almost back to normal again, the tension all but gone.

"If you're waiting for me to tell you how much I weigh, you can just forget it. And I don't even talk Texas."

Laughing, he hefted her, giving an exaggerated groan of relief when he put her down. Lu moved away from him. As long as they were touching, there was always the danger that the sparks might ignite the dangerously combustive atmosphere between them. Next time she might not be so lucky.

Or unlucky. Depending on the point of view. Hers had become so badly distorted lately that she hardly knew which end was up. "Rex, it's past time I was getting back to town. I have to shower and change and get something to eat before I open the gallery at one, not that anyone much comes this time of year. No one interested in art, that is. It's the air conditioning they're after."

"Start charging vent rent."

She shoved back her hair and managed a creditable laugh. It seemed they'd both survived a near miss. "Good idea."

"Hey, don't forget, I promised to cook your catch for you. You wouldn't want all that cooking oil and cornmeal to go to waste, would you?"

"How are you as a short-order cook? We'll have to hurry."

"I've got references from some of the best greasy spoons in five states."

"Wow! Add that to the fact you let slip that you weigh 212, and I'm really getting to know you, right?" Lu teased.

While Rex built a fire in the circle of rocks, Lu released the worms in a damp place near the pond. She sat in the shade of a feathery locust while he dressed the fish. She'd offered to do it, but he'd insisted, leaving her free to admire the smooth efficiency of his movements and the line of his tall, muscular body as he climbed the hill to where she waited. He was far from handsome in the classical sense, and he certainly wasn't the most urbane man she'd ever met. Nor even a great conversationalist. What he *didn't* say took up more space than what he *did* say. So what was it about him that made her react the way she had?

Her emotions had been totally out of control ever since she'd met him, like a runaway truck on a narrow mountain road. As far as she could see, there was little chance for improvement until he was gone from this valley and she could pull herself back together again.

"Now for the treat of your young sheltered life, ma'am," Rex promised, the Texas drawl back in effect. "What would you like to drink? There's a cooler in the van with just about anything your little heart might desire."

"My little heart wants a glass of iced tea. With lemon and sugar."

His face fell. "I didn't see any of that at the convenience store. Does it come in cans?"

Not for the first time, Lu felt a hand close around her heart and squeeze until it hurt. "I was only teasing," she said gently. "Anything cold will be fine."

The first fish sizzled in the frying pan, and Rex squatted beside the fire, sweat gleaming on his bare back. "I'll fetch us a couple of drinks as soon as I get the rest of these things on cooking."

"Let me. What do you want—beer?"

"Buttermilk. There are glasses in the locker over the sink."

The van had been designed as a camper, but converted to a mobile office. Lu had glanced in the back, but Rex hadn't offered her the grand tour. Perhaps things were progressing, after all. Although to what end, she couldn't have said.

Sometime later they both lay back in the shade, replete after a delicious, completely unbalanced meal of fish, bread and fried potatoes. "For such a lousy fisherman, you're not a bad cook," she observed drowsily. "Where'd you get all these references you mentioned?"

"Oh—here and there. You know how it is."

"Ask a direct question and you get a direct runaround," she said dryly. "You're going to have to pick me up and pour me into the van. It's less than an hour before I have to open the gallery, and the way I feel now, I could sleep a solid week."

"Siesta time. Good solid biological basis for it, only I forget now what it is." The sun outside their small circle of shade turned everything to blistering heatwaves. Even the lake lay still and dusty under the pall of the noonday sun.

"Too hot even to swim," Lu murmured. "I'm so full of fish, I'd probably sink, anyway."

"Too hot for most everything," Rex rumbled softly, his eyes half closed.

She caught the gleam of his gaze on her, and her heart leaped like a bass after a mayfly. Really, she was going to have to take herself in hand before she did something irrevocably foolish. It was all very well for a man who could take what he wanted and then move on, but she had an idea she would never get off so lightly.

Nothing was said of her promise last night to have dinner with him again. They drove home in sleepy silence just as church was letting out. Lu climbed down from the van unaided. "That's Lana Potts, the woman in the flowered hat who's standing out on her front porch staring at us."

"Is that a problem?"

"She was my Sunday school teacher. When they finally get around to forming the Lu Lavender Steering Committee, she'll be the chairman. She's been practicing for years."

"You going to get a lecture on the evils of tooling around town with strange men?" Frankly Rex found it rather hard to believe any woman Lu's age would give a damn what her neighbors thought.

"Tooling around and fishing on Sunday. Not to mention that little demonstration on the porch last night when you brought me home." She slipped him a teasing smile. "I'm afraid I'm really in for it now."

"All of a sudden, I'm feeling pretty generous. Why don't we give Miz Potts something to steam up her spectacles?"

Before Lu could react, Rex reached for her, and there in broad daylight, in full view of anyone who happened to be watching, he proceeded to kiss her half out of her mind.

It never even occurred to Lu to protest. Lana Potts was the last thing on her mind. Standing on tiptoe beside the van, she wound her arms around his neck and gave back as good as she got.

Light-years later, when she came back down to earth to find herself standing on the sidewalk in front of her own house, she shook her head in disbelief. "Oh, for goodness' sakes, Rex, that was inexcusable."

"Yes, ma'am, I do believe you're right." He smiled lazily, but for just a moment Lu thought she caught a glimpse of something more than playfulness in his eyes.

Five

Rex watched as she disappeared inside the tall, prim house with its gables and fancy siding, its gingerbread and leaded windows. The differences between them had never been so clearly spelled out. She was quality, family, background, security. She might gripe about neighbors who minded her business, but it was something she took for granted. People around her who cared what happened to her.

After a moment, Rex started the van and headed out toward the Peacock Motel. Maybe it was time he was winding up this job and moving on. What was it they said about rolling stones? First thing he knew, he'd be gathering moss.

Of all times for the phone to ring, when she had less than an hour to make herself presentable! Lu reached for the annoying instrument with one hand while she continued to brush her hair with the other, but on hearing the voice of her best friend, she let the hair brush clatter to the floor.

"Katie? Where are you calling from? Are you back home already? What's the matter, did Homer get antsy?"

"That's one way of putting it," said her best friend, her voice several notes higher than normal, and with a tightness that brought a quick frown to Lu's face. Katie and Homer Mangum were the only two friends who hadn't drifted away after the initial shock of Andrew's death. Their circle of friends had been small, for Andrew had been something of a snob, and they'd never been people Lu would have been drawn to alone.

The Mangums were the exception. Homer was a writer and Katie, earthy, practical and witty, was a highly successful agent for some of the top craftsmen in the area, selling to outlets all over the country. Katie and Lu had been best friends since Lu's first disastrous dinner party, when the quiche had been runny, the salad limp and the rest of the menu no better.

"Come on, what's wrong," Lu coaxed. She had exactly twenty-seven minutes until time to hang out the Open sign. The gallery could wait. "Someone stole your credit cards? You and Homer have discovered that four weeks in a three-room cottage for two is a little too much togetherness?"

"How about three weeks for one in the cottage and three weeks for two in a damned hotel in Bar Harbor?"

"Katie, are you trying to tell me something?" Lu had retrieved the hairbrush. Now it slid from her lap to the floor again. She had a feeling she wasn't going to like this at all, yet she couldn't exactly say she was surprised. Homer had been one of the first to offer none-too-subtle "comfort" soon after Andrew's death. She'd told him he was drunk, and though they'd both known he wasn't, they'd both pretended it was true. Neither of them had mentioned it again.

"He's left me. And, Lu, I don't know what I'm going to do! I keep thinking he'll walk through the door any minute now, but he's got this—this *creature* with him—some college kid with hair down to *here!*"

"Oh, no..."

"Oh, yes. Lu, what did you do after Andrew—how did you handle it? God, at least Andrew didn't dump you. I feel so rotten! Intellectually I know I'm an intelligent, attractive woman, so why do I feel so worthless?"

"Katie, listen to me, you're the same woman you were before. Homer's going through one of those things men go through when they see middle age staring them in the face. It's his problem, not yours."

"Did Andrew?"

"Go through that stage? Honey, you have to remember that Andrew was almost forty when we were married. Maybe *I* was his solution to the midlife crisis, I don't know."

"I'll be thirty-eight next month, dammit—that's no time to be starting over!"

No time to be starting over. The words echoed in Lu's mind. When a woman had had one good marriage, when she had a career and a home and friends—and even irritating, meddlesome neighbors who would nevertheless be the first to come rushing to the rescue if she were ever in real trouble, how could she risk losing it all for a something that could be over before she even knew it?

"Lu? Sorry to be such a pain. So how's it going? Hector still threatening to pin fig leaves on all your nudes?"

"Does anything ever change around here?" Lu countered. She wanted to tell her best friend about Rex, desperately needed a sounding board, but how could she even bring up the fact that she was on the verge of falling in love again when Katie was sitting up in Maine alone in a cottage for two?

"Did he take the car?" Lu asked.

"No, I still have it, and most of the credit cards."

"So why not come home and leave him to twist in the breeze?"

Katie laughed. It was a poor effort, but it was better than nothing. "Maybe I'll tour a few craft studios around here. I could broaden my horizons now that I'm not tied down to that picturesque pile of termite-eaten logs."

Both Katie and Lu had moved into their husbands' family homes. At least Lu's had already had indoor plumbing and central heat. "Keep me posted, will you?"

She was several minutes late getting downstairs to hang out the Open sign. The Hancock sisters, Maude and Mable, were waiting, and before she could usher them inside, Rex arrived. The younger sister was telling her all about a perfectly darling drawing of a squirrel in striped pajamas they'd just had framed, and Lu's fixed smile was still in place when Rex joined them.

"What are you doing here?" she whispered tersely.

"We keep telling Tallulah that she really should have some of our cute little animal drawings in her gallery. My, the children would just love them."

Rex smiled and nodded, and Lu watched the two women flush and simper as they smoothed skirts and patted tightly curled gray hair. If his smile had the same effect on them as it had on her, their corset stays would soon be welded together.

"I'm sure that— Of course, the collection is..." She sighed, wondering how to discourage them without hurting their feelings. She'd seen their drawings. They were dreadful! Even *she* could tell that much.

"What Miz Lavender is trying to say," Rex put in smoothly, "is that a public collection like this can't just snap up anything it likes without going through a whole lot of red tape. You know how it is, ladies—the government has its fingers in everything these days."

"Oh, my, yes," Miss Maude said, beaming.

"Why, I should say so," chimed in Miss Mabel. "All those forms—Medicare, social security, taxes..."

Lu didn't know whether to laugh or to shove him out the door. "I suppose you came to see the Tennisson? Didn't I hear someone say Mr. Tennisson was your nephew?"

"Arnie is the son of our cousin over near Shatley Springs," Maude Hancock corrected.

"Artistic talent always did run in Mama's side of the family," Mabel reminded her, in case she'd forgotten their drawings. "My, it's always so nice and cool in here, isn't it?" With a delicate gesture, she plucked her navy-and-white polka-dot skirt away from her plump thighs.

As soon as they disappeared from the foyer, Lu turned back to Rex. He was standing in the door of the smallest room, pretending to study an exhibit of mountain landscapes. He'd obviously showered and changed, because his hair wasn't even dry yet. Lu knew for a fact that it took as least twenty minutes each way to drive out to the Peacock.

She tried to sound impatient and ended up sounding breathless instead. "What did you want here, Rex?"

With all the innocence of a child caught raiding the cookie jar, he turned to stare at her. "Want? What makes you think I want anything? This place is open to the public, isn't it? And like the lady said, it's nice and cool in here."

"Rex," Lu said warningly. Dammit, he was pressuring her and she needed time to think. After talking to Katie, she *definitely* needed more time to think.

"Besides, you told me yourself that there wasn't a whole lot to do around these parts. Church is over, I've already had lunch and the fish aren't biting."

Lu closed her eyes and prayed for patience. How on earth had she gotten herself mixed up with this...this Texas conman? This refugee from a grade-B western who could beguile the heart right out of her body with one of his slow, sweet smiles? "Well...all right. Look all you want to, but please don't get me in any more trouble with my neighbors than I already am."

"Ma'am, all in the world I'm lookin' for is a mite of culture and a tad of air conditioning, honest. You've got the best outfit around these parts, they tell me. Takes a heap o' coolin' to handle one of these old houses."

She had to laugh. A family came in and wandered over to the middle room, staying close to the vents. He nodded, a knowing look on his face. "See? Told you you ought to be charging vent rent. You're not a very sharp businesswoman, Miz Lavender."

"Rex, you're shameless. If you're going to hang around, you could at least pretend to be interested in the paintings."

"I think we both know what I'm interested in, Lu." He reached out to touch a curl that had sprung loose from the French braid that was supposed to keep her hair up off her neck.

"Do we?" she asked, suddenly feeling terribly vulnerable. Things were moving too fast. She was a small-town woman who'd never been exposed to anyone even faintly like Rex Jones before. For a little while she'd been swept along in his wake, but after talking to Katie, whose whole world had just collapsed, the safe, the dull and familiar suddenly seemed very desirable.

"Lu? Should I have stayed away, then?" His hand had fallen from her hair to her shoulders, and now one finger traced the tendon at the side of her neck above the lace collar of her voile dress.

She stepped back, feeling the brush of his fingers all the way to the soles of her feet. It was uncanny, the effect his touch had on her nerves. "That might have been best," she said. The words held little conviction, even to her own ears.

"You don't believe that any more than I do, Lu. Okay, so maybe we don't know each other very well. Let's give it a chance." His gaze drifted down to her breasts. The tip of his tongue showed briefly as he caught his lower lip with a square white tooth. The chipped one. She all but groaned aloud.

"Lu, I've got two jobs waiting to consider, and I don't want to leave here without some understanding," Rex said softly, his voice suddenly urgent. He moved closer, and she stopped breathing altogether.

The Hancock sisters emerged, their faces tight with disapproval. Grateful for the reprieve, Lu turned away. "What did you think of Arnie's painting?"

"My, it certainly is ugly, isn't it? Why in the world would anyone want to hang a thing like that on the wall? Now you take our little animal children," Miss Maude said. "Everybody likes those."

"Poor boy." Miss Mabel shook her head. "But then, he's only a third cousin once removed."

There was no more time to talk. Visitors continued to wander in and out all afternoon, mostly locals with the occasional tourist. Parrish Falls was hardly a resort area—it wasn't even considered quaint—but there were always the curious who liked to get off the beaten path. And Parrish Falls was definitely that.

Rex was a model of decorum. Lu almost wished he'd resort to his usual outrageous self. She didn't trust him on his best behavior, and she certainly didn't trust him on his worst.

How on earth could she even *think* she loved a man she couldn't trust? Still, Katie had trusted Homer, and look what had happened to her.

Lu was forced to give her spiel about Arnold Bingham Tennisson and the forces that shaped his life's work three separate times, and each time it grew more difficult, with Rex taking in every word.

She avoided looking at him, but she could feel his presence in the room, like a prowling tiger newly released from his cage. He made her acutely nervous, but she was honest enough to admit that if he'd left, she would have been in even worse shape.

After a while, she got so she could almost ignore him. When one of the local boys, egged on by friends, had blurted out a question concerning the differences between a nude and a "nekkid" lady, she hadn't turned a hair. A few minutes later, she calmly routed two underage smokers from the storage closet, pointed out the No Smoking sign and asked if they would mind helping her to unstick a painted-shut window. Afterward, reminding them that smoking around so much paint and paper could be dangerous, she suggested that from now on they go out on the front porch whenever they felt the urge to light up, knowing that would put an end to it.

At half-past three, there was a lull. She located Rex in the smallest gallery and joined him there. "Rex, I've been thinking. Maybe we'd better let well enough alone."

"Meaning?" He turned from the paintings he'd been examining, a trio of colorful primitives.

"Meaning—well, that we don't really have anything in common, do we? There doesn't seem to be a whole lot of future in carrying on this...I mean, our..."

"In carrying on?"

"Exactly," she snapped. "You said yourself you'll be moving on any day now. I suppose you're used to...ah, diversions when you're on the road, but Rex, I don't think I'm cut out to be a diversion."

"I like these things," he said, nodding to the paintings. "Are they any good?"

"What?" It took her a moment to make the shift, but then she picked up her cue. They were getting too personal. Talking about his taste in art was one thing, but talking about his taste in—diversions—was quite another.

"They happen to be my personal favorites, too," she said coolly. "The artist was completely untrained. She started out using food coloring and then house paint before she got her first set of oils."

"Now that's what I'd call a happy bunch of people," Rex said thoughtfully. He read off the title. *"All Day Singing and Dinner on the Ground.* Even sounds happy, doesn't it?"

Unthinking, Lu moved a step closer to his side, touched in spite of herself by a note that was almost wistful. She was being fanciful, of course. *Wistful* was the very last word anyone would think of using to describe a man like Rex Jones.

As he continued to examine the paintings, she studied his irregular profile, the high forehead under a sheaf of unruly hair, the crooked nose, the jaw that could have been chiseled from granite. He was serious.

Something inside her began to crumble, and she braced herself against his insidious charm. Now, why on earth should the reaction of a tough-looking stranger to a picture of a group of people frolicking around a country church make her want to take him into her arms and hold him close?

Abruptly she turned away. "I like this one, too," she said a bit gruffly.

Rex turned his attention to the smallest canvas, depicting a group of women of all ages seated around a quilting frame in an unfinished attic room. "*Mama's Quilting Bee For Sister's Wedding*," he noted. And after a moment added, "I'd like to meet the artist. She must be quite a lady."

He really meant it! "I'm sorry," Lu said. "She died several years ago. She was eighty-seven and still painting." Without thinking, she reached for his hand and laced her fingers through his. "Miss Lilly would have loved you. She probably would have painted you."

She could visualize the artist's version of Rex's rawboned frame and shaggy, sun-bleached hair as he chopped wood or plowed a rocky, sloping field behind a team of mules. He'd be the perfect model for the rugged woodsman, the pioneer, the frontiersman.

Together, they wandered in to stand before the Tennisson. "Now here we have a classical case of hometown boy makes good in big city," she said playfully, assuming her role as docent as a defense against the painful closeness she'd felt a moment before. "At the moment, no one seems to know for sure if it's all a hoax or retribution for Arnie's having been held back in school two years in a row or a diabolical plot to overthrow the governments of the free world."

Rex chuckled. "Which theory do you subscribe to?"

"I'm not sure. I wouldn't go so far as to fine him for polluting the atmosphere, like Mr. Tate suggested, but I probably won't miss the thing when the exhibit ends next month, either. What about you? Care to add your critique?"

She heard the sound of a car door outside. She hadn't wanted Rex here; she certainly hadn't wanted to be alone with him so soon after Katie's upsetting news, not until she'd had time to reexamine her own position. But now that someone else was coming through the front gate, she felt an irrational desire to rush out and flip over the Closed sign on the door. She tried to tug her hand from his.

"I don't rightly believe I can comment, ma'am," Rex said with that slow, endearing grin of his. He turned his hand so that he was cupping her fist in his palm, his thumb smoothing the skin on the inside of her wrist. "Truth is, I don't happen to speak the man's language. Be a shame to misjudge him on account of we don't see things from the same side of the fence, so to speak."

Once more Lu felt something reach inside her and tighten around her heart. It occurred to her that for a man whose background remained such a mystery, he was someone she was coming to know an awful lot about.

She might not know who his parents were and where he'd gone to school, but she did know that he was innately fair. He might be solvent or up to his ears in debt, but there was a wealth of kindness in him. There was a gentleness about him that she suspected he considered a weakness.

And he was shy. Why else would he hide behind those outrageous mannerisms?

"Good evening, Tallulah."

Fixing a smile on her face, Lu turned to greet Hector. He was late. As a rule he was there when the doors opened and stayed until the bitter end. "Nice of you to stop by, Hector. You've met Rex Jones, I believe?"

Another group came in while the three of them stood awkwardly in the doorway. Rex murmured a general greeting and edged toward the door. "Perryman," he acknowledged. "I'll be seein' you, ma'am. Thanks for showin' me Miss Lilly's pictures. Pick o' the litter, I'd say."

He left then, and ignoring the newcomers, Lu stared after him. It was only a quarter of four, but already the sky had grown dull.

Six

"Do you have a grill?"

"Rex?" Lu panted. She was breathless from having raced for the phone after showing her last visitors out, thinking it was Katie calling back to talk now that the gallery was closed. "Rex! Would you mind telling me what's going on?"

"I'm trying to arrange supper. You promised me last night, remember?"

"I've hardly had time to forget, with you underfoot every minute since."

There was a long silence, long enough for Lu to regret her hasty words. "Maybe I'd better take a hike and let you get some rest then," he said quietly.

She didn't want him to take a hike! Not unless she could take it with him. "No, please—I didn't mean that. I'm tired, but I'm also starved. What sort of grill?"

"One that'll hold a couple of slabs of beef. I'll pick up charcoal on the way into town."

"What can I do? Salad? Iced tea? Dessert?"

"Lie down and put your feet up. I'll take care of everything."

"Let me make us salads, at least." Suddenly she wasn't nearly as tired as she'd been only moments before. It was probably a symptom of something she didn't care to delve into at the moment.

"Whatever you want to do—just don't wear yourself out in the kitchen. I can pick up a can of pork and beans when I get the charcoal, if you insist on a vegetable."

"I don't know how you managed to grow so big, if that's your idea of a balanced diet," she teased.

"Beans are vegetables, aren't they?"

On the verge of making a remark about the things his mother had never taught him, Lu decided to leave well enough alone. By the time she heard Rex arrive, she had managed to change out of her lace-collared dress and into a yellow sundress and sandals and had washed the store-bought lettuce and one of the last of her tomatoes.

"That was fast. Rex, you didn't have to do this. After all, you fed me breakfast and cooked my lunch. Anyone would think you'd taken me on to raise." He was laden down with a sack of charcoal and a brown grocery bag from which protruded a loaf of French bread. In the process of taking it from him, Lu feasted her gaze on the laughing hazel eyes that were bracketed by crows-feet, the angular planes of his tanned face and the jaw that could only be called stubborn.

The man was tough as old boots and looked it, she reminded herself. So why did he invariably have this effect on her? Why did she find so much pleasure in being with him? A man like that could never be satisfied to stay in one place for long, and her whole life was tied up in Parrish Falls. Her responsibilities were here.

"Hope you liked that wine we had last night," Rex said as he glanced around at the cheerful yellow-and-white kitchen with its old-fashioned high ceiling and tall cabinets. "We're having a repeat."

Lu removed the bottle of red wine from the sack. "And I hope you didn't do anything grossly illegal. I happen to know that stores around here don't sell beer or wine on Sundays."

"Nope." Rex picked up the freshly scoured grill and headed for the back door. "Just a mite of bartering."

Lu grabbed a folded tablecloth, a metal platter and a cooking fork, and hurried after him. There hadn't been time to scrub the old picnic table out under the oak tree, but with a clean tablecloth it would serve well enough. "You bartered for wine? I think that's probably even worse," she said, laughing.

"Remember that copper tree mixed in with the real ones at the restaurant last night? It's supposed to be a fountain, but I noticed last night that it wasn't working and the carpet around it was watermarked."

Perched on one of the weathered, lichen-covered benches, Lu watched him heap charcoal in the brick fireplace, pour fluid on it and light it. "Is all this leading up to something?"

"You mean the steak dinner?"

"I mean the story."

"Oh. Oh, yeah—well, anyhow, I dropped in on the way out to the Peacock to see if I could get us reservations for tonight, and the manager and that winefellow with the funny accent were tinkering with the thing. First thing you know, I was tinkering, too. Whoever put the thing together knew a lot more about brazing metal than he did about plumbing. Upshot of the deal was that we ended up fixing it so that it flows like a spigot, with no leaks, no dam-ups, and no overshoots."

"And all this explains the wine?"

"The steak *and* the wine. Since I'm not licensed as a plumber, I couldn't very well charge for my labor. Just my luck they wanted to show their appreciation with a couple of pounds of beef and a bottle of Cabernet Sauvignon."

Lu pursed her lips. "Just your luck," she echoed soberly. "What about the reservations?"

He tugged at his open collar. "Reservations? Oh, yeah—they were all booked up for tonight. Just my luck." Brushing his hands together, Rex came and stood before her, so close she could see the glints of mischief in his eyes. "Yes, ma'am—just my luck," he drawled softly, reaching for her.

He was incredibly gentle for a man so strong. It was as if he was afraid of hurting her. He brushed his mouth over hers again and again, until she could have died for a taste of the sweetness of him. When she felt the flicker of his tongue, she moaned softly in her throat, and as if it were the signal he'd been waiting for, he deepened the kiss until she was reeling.

Several minutes later he released her. She stood there swaying, dusty handprints on her back, a dazed look on her face and a cooking fork dangling from one hand. Carefully she laid it on the table by the grill. Lifting her hand, she touched his mouth and then her own with her fingertips. How was it possible for the coming together of two sets of lips to have such a cataclysmic effect on any human being?

"Rex, I'm not quite sure what's going on here, but I don't think I'm ready for it," she whispered.

"That's kinda like jumping off the cliff and then having second thoughts, isn't it? Once you get a little momentum, it's hard to turn back." The pupils of his eyes had almost engulfed the green-gold irises. She was drowning in their depths.

"Would you mind if we tried?" she whispered. "Or at least took it a bit slower?"

"Is that what you want?"

A chorus of insects tuned up, enveloping them in the sound. "No, but it's what I think best. You bring out a part of me I don't even recognize," she confessed. They stood close. Not touching, but close enough so that she caught a drift of woodsy fragrance mingled with his healthy masculine scent. Under the best of circumstances, she knew she wasn't up to handling something this explosive. Cocooned together in the rich lavender-green ambience of a spent day, she knew she hadn't a prayer. "Rex, give me time, will you? I've never done anything like this before."

He deliberately chose to misunderstand her. "Never grilled steaks?"

Impatiently she waved away his flippant response. "You know very well what I'm talking about. I suppose it's nothing new for you. Any man who travels around as much as you do must be accustomed to... accustomed to—"

"Accustomed to what, Miz Lavender? To trackin' down lonesome young widows and movin' in on 'em? Is that what you figure this is?"

Hearing the rough edge to his voice, Lu was thoroughly ashamed of herself. "I'm sorry, Rex. That was a terrible thing to imply."

Turning away, he adjusted the grill over the charcoal. "Is that really what you think, Lu?"

"No." Her hesitation was barely noticeable. "I don't think that at all. Rex, it's not that I don't trust you—I do, even though I hardly know you at all. I can't pretend I'm not attracted to you. Rather a lot," she added hesitantly, glancing up to see if her words had made any visible impact. She'd practically admitted she was in love with the man, but if he felt anything at all, it was another of his well-kept secrets. "Dammit, I'm probably doing everything all wrong! I told you I was inexperienced at this sort of thing, and I meant it. I've never been what you might call a social butterfly."

"A social butterfly," he repeated, his granite visage allowing a slow smile to break through. "Lu, do you think I don't know that? Did you think I couldn't take one look at you and know right off just how rare and special you were?"

Lu dropped down onto one of the benches, oblivious to the grime, the lichen and the debris left by feeding birds and squirrels. "Don't make fun of me, Rex. I'm thirty-seven years old. I was married for eleven years. I'm reasonably intelligent, I've always been considered capable enough—at least capable of taking care of myself. But now, all of a sudden, I can't think straight. I can't seem to keep my mind on what I'm supposed to be doing. I've got all these—uh, funny feelings, and it's—well, it's scary!"

Was it only her imagination, or did she sound an awful lot like Katie? But that didn't make sense. Katie was in a state of near panic because she'd *lost* a man. Lu was falling apart because she'd *found* one!

Idly Rex twisted a fallen oak twig between thumb and forefinger, his attention seemingly on the cluster of green acorns. He made no comment, and Lu felt compelled to fill the silence.

"You have to understand that my grandparents were already in their sixties when I came to live with them. I come from a long line of late bloomers and only children, which is probably why I never dated very much until I went off to school. And then I met Andrew."

Lu searched his profile for a clue as to his reaction. She wasn't good at introspection—never had been. She was even worse at trying to explain feelings that she was at a loss to understand herself. With Andrew it had been different. She'd been young and gauche, but he hadn't expected her to be otherwise. This time she didn't have that excuse.

"All I'm trying to say is that I went from my grandparents' home to a girls' dorm and from there to my marriage without a lot of freedom to experiment along the way. I had to study very hard in school and work, too, because the insurance my parents left didn't stretch all that far. So you see, there wasn't time for any, uh, hanky-panky. It isn't that I don't want to, Rex. I just don't feel very sure of myself."

"Is that what you think I'm offering you? *Hanky-panky?*"

"No, of course not. Well, I don't know," she amended. "Isn't it?"

"What do you want from me, Lu?"

She stared down at the toe of her sandal. Dammit, hadn't he heard a single word she'd said? She'd practically told him she was willing to have an affair. Not in so many words, perhaps, but surely he'd known what she was getting at. She might have her doubts; she might not be up on the protocol in such situations, but one thing she *did* know—she wanted as much of him as he was willing to share with her. She'd worry about tomorrow...tomorrow.

Could she have misread the signs? Either that or she'd turned him off with her little confession. From embarrassment she plunged directly to misery.

The fire blazed fitfully, and Rex leaned against a tree trunk, hooking his foot up behind him. He watched the play of expressions on her face, guessing something of her uncertainty. Hell, he felt it, too.

He'd known all along he had no business messing up her life. If he was smart, he would walk out right now, before he got in any deeper. Every word she said only told him what he'd known from the first. They were as different as fire and ice and they would destroy each other before they were done. All his life he'd made the mistake of wanting things he was never meant to have. He'd never had a home of his home, so he'd married Kelli when he was nineteen and she was a year younger. He'd wanted children, so he'd worked construction during the day and gone to school nights to prepare for the day when they could afford them.

And then the nightmare had come. Before his twenty-first birthday, it had all blown up in his face. The marriage, the dreams, school, his job. Oh, yes, his wonderful job and his brand-new promotion. It had just about destroyed him.

"Fire's almost ready," he said, levering himself away from the rough bark. He stretched his arms over his head, yawning. "Been too hot to sleep lately, hasn't it? Why don't we toss the steaks on now and make an early night of it? I've got me one hellacious headache out at Davis. Hate to break the news to them, but short of a major overhaul, there's no easy way to solve their problems."

Lu hiccupped. Immediately she jumped up and made a show of brushing off the table and spreading the tablecloth, wishing she'd never seen or heard of a sweet-talking Texan with a chipped-tooth grin. *Hiccup.* "Did I light the oven? The bread—I'll put it in and bring out the steaks. Oh, and the salad! Is iced tea all right? Oh, no, we have the wine." *Hiccup!*

Rex watched her scurry into the house, heard the screen door slam behind her and swore. Dammit, now he'd hurt her feelings. Embarrassed her at the very

least. He'd known from the start where that little
confession of hers had been headed, and something in
him—some shred of decency, or maybe just a scrap of
survival instinct—had warned him to back off before
he got in any deeper.

If it wasn't already too late.

Lightning flashed in the distance, and several moments later, thunder rumbled. This had been one hell
of an August, any way you looked at it. Another few
days, a week at best, and he could shake the dust of
this place off his boots for good and get on with the
next challenge. The Delaware job might be bigger, but
he thought he would head for Maine. He had a feeling he was going to need to go a long, long way to
forget what he'd found in Parrish Falls, North Carolina.

By the time Lu emerged with the steaks, her com-
posure was largely intact. She was good at facades.
That came with practice. A damp paper towel had
cooled off her face and throat, but she could still feel
the tight curls of hair sticking to the back of her neck.
The hiccups were over, thanks to ten tiny sips of
orange juice and a bit of deep breathing. Otherwise
known as sighing.

"Coals about right?" she asked cheerfully. "Looks
like we might just have time to get the steaks up to
medium rare before the storm gets here. If we have to,
we can grab the platter and run for the back door."
With a little more practice, she might be good at this.

The rain struck just as Rex forked the last strip of
beef onto the heated platter. He took that while Lu

rolled up tablecloth, gingham napkins, silverware and all, and they dashed for the kitchen.

"Thank goodness I hadn't brought out the salads yet," she gasped, blotting her eyes on a corner of the tablecloth.

"Or poured the wine." Silverware clattered to the floor. "Here, let me take that stuff before you slice off a toe." He removed the wadded bundle from her arms, his eyes crinkling into a heart-melting smile. A blast of thunder split the air just as the lights flickered, and Lu jumped.

"Better change into something dry," he said gruffly. "The steaks are still sizzling. They'll keep if you get a move on."

Lu hurried back into the kitchen a few minutes later wearing white linen slacks and a pink cotton pullover. "I always heard North Carolina was right up there at the top of the list when it came to thunderstorms." The lights flickered again as the storm lowered its full fury over the narrow valley, and she shivered. "It's a distinction I could do without."

There was a confusion of noise outside, and this time the lights flickered, dimmed and went out altogether. Lu moved closer to Rex's side. "That sounded like a tree going down. There was a dead branch on that big oak down the street that's been threatening to fall for months."

"Probably took a few lines with it. Meanwhile, we might as well enjoy a little candlelight with our dinner." Rex peered through the windows, but in the pitch darkness, there was little to see.

"Candlelight and wine—now all we need is music." And then she could have kicked herself. They'd both decided to leave romance *out* of it. At least, he'd decided and she'd agreed, knowing it was the smart thing to do. "I'll see if I have a candle. I usually keep a few stubs on hand for times like this."

Rex offered to get a flashlight from the van, but she told him she knew exactly where she kept them. Wise, practical Tallulah, she jeered silently.

By feel she located two candles in a drawer filled with string, lids that didn't fit anything and out-of-date store coupons. She sat them in metal jar lids rather than dig out the cut-glass candelabra with all the prisms that had been prized by generations of Lavenders.

The steaks were barely warm by the time they got around to eating, but neither of them seemed to notice. Rex quickly drained his wineglass and refilled it. Lu toyed with her steak knife, absently stroking the rounded handle with her thumb. The storm grew even noisier, and Rex got up and began to prowl, checking windows. It was growing increasingly stuffy without the air conditioner.

Instead of returning to his chair, he moved to stand behind hers. He didn't speak. He didn't touch her. Finally Lu's knife clattered to the table, and she twisted around to glare up at him. "For heaven's sake, sit down. You're making me nervous! Don't tell me you're afraid of thunderstorms."

"Let's just say that as an electrical engineer, I have a healthy respect for all that unharnessed voltage."

"Well, as a layman, so do I, but since this house is bristling with some of the fanciest lightning rods you'll ever see anywhere, I can respect the stuff without being paranoid."

"Good to know. Let's just hope that whoever installed 'em knew enough to ground 'em right. Glass balls and curlicues are only good for warding off witches and werewolves."

Lu grinned, the mention of witches and werewolves having deflected some of the tension that had risen to almost unbearable levels.

"Did I ever tell you about the time I was caught in an apple tree in a thunderstorm?" He moved away to stand beside the back door, and she flexed her shoulders in relief. He was worse than the lightning!

"You've never told me anything I didn't have to pry out of you with a crowbar. What were you doing in an apple tree—stealing apples?"

"Why do you think I was so scared? I'd been warned a couple of hundred times already that the good Lord was going to knock my back teeth down my throat if I didn't change my ways. I thought for sure he'd caught me dead to rights that day."

She had to laugh. Pushing back her plate, she stood, and it seemed only natural when Rex draped an arm across her shoulders and led her into the cluttered parlor. "I refuse to wash dishes by candlelight," he said in excuse, and Lu was perfectly willing to go along with it.

The streetlight that normally shone through the window was out, but there was a flickering brightness that lit the way to the old horsehair sofa. "The blue chair's more comfortable.'' Safer, too, she added silently. "I've always hated this monstrosity, but Andrew has a cousin over near Elkin who pops in at unexpected times to take inventory of all the family relics. I think she's always a little surprised when I haven't pawned the lot and spent it all on riotous living.''

Chuckling softly, Rex sat down and pulled her beside him, drawing her against his side so that her head was cushioned against his shoulder. She resisted only for a moment. Okay, so they'd decided to eat their steaks and call it quits, she rationalized. No point in being fanatical about it. With a few minor adjustments, she had to admit that the old sofa had never felt so good.

"Comfortable, Miz Lavender?"

"Perfectly, Mr. Jones.''

"Mmm, reckon it'll do to ride out the storm, all right.'' He cupped his hand over her shoulder and began to stroke, and there was nothing at all seductive about it. It was merely... nice.

The flickering continued. Lu could almost make believe it was a flickering fire in the small, tile-faced fireplace—*their* fireplace—and they were snowed in together. It was a harmless-enough dream, she told herself. What harm could there be in a simple dream, as long as you knew that that's all it was?

Beneath her cheek, Rex's heart beat with reassuring steadiness. He was even harder than the sofa, but the hardness wasn't at all uncomfortable, not when she fitted into the hollows of his body as if they'd been designed as two parts of a whole.

Bravely Lu faced a few facts. She wanted him more than she'd ever have believed she could want any man not her husband. Now that she'd finally accepted that fact, there was no guilt attached to the wanting. It had been six years, after all. Some women didn't even wait six months.

But the feeling had to be mutual. There had to be caring and respect on both sides, or it would never work, not for her. "About what you were saying earlier," she began tentatively. "Just before the storm struck."

"About stealing apples, you mean? Honey, I might be hardheaded, but even *I* learn eventually. I got away that time with no more than a bellyache, but be damned if I'm going to tackle a wet iron fence with twenty-three thousand volts running through it. I can take a hint."

"What are you talking about?" She tried to get up, but he held her in place.

"Power line's down. Where'd you think all the fireworks were coming from—shorted-out lighting bugs?"

The acceleration in his heartbeat couldn't have been caused by the small exertion of dragging her back down to his side. Lu twisted around to peer up at his profile. "Well, *do* something! Call someone. *You're* the expert."

"I'm doing what any good citizen would do in my position, and that's keeping an innocent bystander out of harm's way. Put your feet up, darlin', turn around this way and get comfortable. No tellin' how long it'll be before the power crews get this mess untangled."

"Now look here, Rex Jones, you're the one who decided to call this thing off. Are you trying to tell me now that you've changed your mind *again?*"

"What thing was that, ma'am?" he asked, maddeningly cool.

"You know damned well what thing! I was all ready to— Well, I practically offered to— You know. Have an affair with you. Only you'd already changed your mind."

Leaning his head back on the carved rosewood frame, Rex closed his eyes. "For all the good it did me," he muttered feelingly. He held her loosely against him, and after a while, Lu began to extricate herself. The arms tightened immediately. "Don't you even know why, honey?"

"I told you my education was spotty in some areas." Her voice sounded almost churlish. Lord, she had all the savoir-faire of a molting turkey!

"Lu, did you ever see something you wanted real bad, even knowing you couldn't afford it, knowing it wasn't the sort of thing you had any business wanting? And you kept right on wanting it all the same, until you talked yourself into thinking maybe you deserved it?"

The stillness in the room grew more intense. Except for rain that beat sullenly against the tall windows, the storm had ended. Lu was acutely aware of the heat generated by two bodies in close proximity, and of the growing tension in the hard muscles beneath her. She spoke, and her voice came out a whisper. "Yes. Lots of times. Doesn't everyone?"

"Some of us learn better. Some of us only think we've learned."

"What was it you wanted so much, Rex?" Her eyes sought his, wanting to know more of this hard, gentle man, this tough, sensitive creature who drew her to him only to push her away.

"You. Other things at other times in my life, but now just you." His laughter held more self-mockery than amusement. "Oh, God, more than all the green apples in all the trees in all the orchards in the world, I wanted you the first time I ever laid eyes on you."

Seven

The silence spun out interminably. Lu forgot to breathe.

"Ah, come on, Lu, you can't be all that surprised. Some things a man can't fake."

"But then, why...?"

"Why am I pulling out?"

She nodded. "I know you wanted me, Rex, and it was mutual, only every time I work up my nerve to do something about it, you start backing away."

"Maybe I'm discovering that I still have a conscience."

"I don't see where conscience comes into it at all. Neither of us is attached. At least I'm not. Are you?"

He shook his head slowly. "No. No strings, no ties, no obligations."

"Then why?" Her voice sounded plaintive, and she did her best to make it firm and decisive. "You're telling me that when one party changes his mind, the other party's supposed to shrug it off as a near miss and forget it ever happened?"

It was difficult to sound firm and decisive when she was being held in his arms, her head cradled in the hollow of his shoulder. Taking a deep breath, Lu gave it another shot. "Is that what you're trying to say? Rex, I'm trying to be very adult about this whole thing, but frankly, I think your rules stink."

"Lu, please—" There were deep lines of stress between his brows, lines that Lu did her best to ignore.

"But then, I warned you, I'm a dead loss at this sort of thing. Better luck with your next... *diversion*."

Rex felt himself going under for the third time. "Lu, in case it hadn't occurred to you, I'm not exactly handling this like some storybook Prince Charming, either. No—don't move. Don't move a muscle, because somewhere along the line, my better judgment took off for parts unknown, and without it..." Air whistled through his teeth as he inhaled sharply.

Lu felt her face growing even warmer as his meaning became embarrassingly clear. There was no way she could ignore the hard evidence of his desire, no way even to pretend she hadn't noticed it.

"Rex, I'm sorry. I don't know how it happened—I honestly didn't intend for you to get all—I mean, for us to get so— Oh, for goodness' sake! Look, I'm sorry! If there's anything I can do..."

Oh, no. She hadn't really said that. Not even the dimmest wit would say something so stupid.

Groaning, Rex lowered his head to her hair. She wasn't sure if he was laughing or crying, and she was afraid to open her mouth again for fear of what might emerge.

"Lu, thanks, but don't make it any tougher on me, will you? For once in my misbegotten existence I'm trying to play fair. The last thing you need is a roughneck like me to barge into your life, destroy all that sweetness and then take off again. Lu, you deserve a hell of a lot more than I could ever offer you."

Lu didn't know what to say. Acting purely on instinct, she lifted her face, and then his mouth was only a breath away from hers. Within moments, she was on her back, with Rex half covering her body, his lips dragging over hers as his tongue probed relentlessly, expressing need, frustration, anger and a hunger that quickly spiraled out of control.

With the power off and the air conditioner down, the heat had grown oppressive. His shirt came off first, and then her pullover. He found the button at her waistband, and soon her slacks were on the floor. Layers of clothing fell unheeded as hot, damp flesh sought hot, damp flesh.

"So sweet—so perfect. Lu, please don't stop me now," Rex said huskily as he knelt over her, reaching for his belt.

Stop him! Dear Lord, that was the last thing she wanted to do. She was drowning in need, wild with a hunger that drove her to take the lead. Timidly at first, her hands covered his, and she took over the task of undressing him. She was clumsy. It was awkward. She'd never undressed another person before. But when Rex would have helped her, she stayed his hands. "Please—I want to do it."

"Ah, darlin', you'd better hurry, then. I'm all yours—what's left of me." His ragged laugh rasped warmly against her throat.

She finished unhooking the buckle and found the tab of his zipper, and he swore softly as her small fingertips fought against the straining pressure to draw it slowly downward. The yellow light from the guttering candles in the kitchen cast eerie shadows on his gleaming chest as he rose above her. Lu, worshiping him with her eyes, slid her hands between the cool flesh of his narrow hips and the warm cotton of his pants and tugged them down over his powerful thighs.

With a guttural sound in the back of his throat, Rex stood, kicked off his boots and stepped out of the remainder of his clothes. Then somehow they were both on the floor, and Lu felt the soft scratchiness of the faded old Persian rug under her back, and then she was conscious of nothing but Rex, his towering strength and the trembling of his hands as they began to explore the aching secrets of her body.

He was incredibly gentle, sensitive to needs she was hardly aware of herself. She'd expected so large a man to be rough, but he was more than she could have dreamed, with her limited experience.

How could she have imagined such a driving, compulsive urgency? She'd never known anything even faintly like the inner storm that had her clinging and pleading, reaching for him with her hands and her thighs and her lips. In the small portion of her mind that was still capable of rational thought, she realized that he was exerting almost superhuman control, and she cried out her impatience.

"Rex, please—I need you!"

"Soon, love, soon," he promised, his voice muffled in the soft dampness of her breasts.

Waiting, waiting, touching, tasting, swirling ever higher. He turned away, and she cried out, but then he came back to cover her with his strength, and this time there was no holding back.

Aeons later, drifting breathlessly down to earth like a shower of spent fireworks, Lu told herself that whatever doubts either of them had had earlier, surely this changed everything. After tonight, how could either of them pretend this was merely a fling, a—a diversion?

Lying close in the darkness, her head pillowed on his shoulder, his arm around her waist, Lu listened as his breathing slowly returned to normal. She thought about the bed upstairs, and her mind veered away. Not yet.

Should she invite him to stay the night? There were things that still had to be resolved, in her mind as well as his. She was only sure of one thing—she didn't want him to leave her soon. Maybe never.

Her arms tightened in an unconscious reflection of her thoughts. She'd thought he was asleep. He wasn't.

"Lu, I want you to know that no matter what happens, I'd never intentionally hurt you," Rex said quietly just as the lights flickered on again.

They talked then, lazily, curled in each other's arms. His defenses for once at a low ebb, Rex told her something of his childhood and his jobs at the docks. "I never eat a shrimp without wondering who headed it. There's a lot to be said for getting an early start with manual labor—teaches you something you don't get out of books."

"I wondered how you developed such nimble hands," Lu said, catching her breath as one of those hands slipped around her waist and began exploring her navel.

"You'd be surprised at all the things I developed— like the ability to make a cozy nest out of nothing more than a skimpy little doohicky and a couple of lumpy pillows..." Scooping the antique silk patchwork throw and two matching quilted cushions from the sofa, he arranged them on the floor without releasing her, and then lowered her onto the jewel-colored silk.

Lu laughed up at him, her eyes drowsy with satisfaction. "All this and a short-order cook, too—you really are a paragon, Mr. Jones."

"That's what I've been telling you, Miz Lavender. In my own modest way, of course."

"Of course," she echoed, brimming with laughter that was swallowed up in a slow, torrid kiss. The moment his lips came down on hers, they were both lost again.

"It's something in the water, isn't it?" he whispered as he buried his face in her throat. "Something all you beautiful, gray-eyed mountain women put in the well water to trap unwary guys like me who happen to be passing through."

"Do you feel trapped, Rex?" The question was asked lightly, but she listened intently for his answer, her hands playing over the corded muscles of his back.

"If I do, it's too late to worry about it now. This is one trap I walked into with both eyes wide open. As far as I'm concerned, you can throw away the key."

Which was practically a declaration, wasn't it? Lu asked herself. The sort of declaration a woman might expect from a man who hid behind an outrageous cowboy act whenever anyone got too close to discovering the real Rex Jones.

It *felt* like a commitment, though Lu had to admit that at the moment, she was in no position to judge.

Rex's eyes burned feverishly as they roamed over her supine body. He knelt beside her there in the stiff cluttered parlor, amid all the stiff Victorian furniture, and began a lingering tour of all the erogenous areas they'd discovered together.

Delighting him with her newfound boldness, she returned the favor, savoring anew the feel of his body, the varying textures of satin, silk and erotic fur; the contrasts—the coolness of his buttocks and the intense heat as her hand strayed over his narrow hips and began to explore further. Dreamily she absorbed the clean musky scent of him and the taste, driving him wild with a slow series of tiny nibbles and long, wet kisses.

The first time had been wonderful. The second time was even more blissful, for Rex had skillfully stripped her of any remaining inhibitions. Lu felt as if she'd only just been born and was experiencing life for the very first time.

"God, Lu, what have you done to me?" Rex groaned as he collapsed and rolled over onto his back. He carried her with him so that she was lying precariously on top of his shuddering body.

"I think it's called love," she ventured. Her whole life seemed to hang suspended as she waited for his response.

A soft snore rumbled in his chest, and she groaned. "In fact, I'm sure it's called love," she whispered against a throbbing pulse in his throat.

Sometime later, she awoke to find him propped on his elbows, leaning over to stare down at her face. "Tired?" he whispered.

"The best kind of tired," she replied, smiling. Whether or not he'd heard her before, surely he had only to look at her to know how she felt. She could no more hide it than she could fly.

They made slow, delicious love again, and sometime after she fell asleep for the last time, Rex laid her on the sofa, covered her with the quilted silk throw and let himself out. Just as the light was beginning to gray the eastern sky, Lu dragged herself upstairs and crawled into bed for a few hours of sleep on a decent surface, knowing that otherwise, she'd have kinks in her back for a week.

Now she lay in her marriage bed and gazed up at the ceiling, a slightly inane grin on her face. Had she actually...?

She had.

How did she feel about it in the cold light of a new day?

Hmm. Happy. A little sore in places, but all in all, rather pleased at how she was taking everything in stride. Contrary to what she'd told Rex last night, it would seem that she was perfectly capable of dealing with an adult relationship in an adult manner. People did this sort of thing every day without demanding declarations, guarantees or commitments.

It weren't as if she were reckless, but after all, no one with a grain of sense rushed into anything these days. There were too many uncertainties. Just look at Katie and Homer. Everyone thought they'd had a perfect marriage. Lu might have had a few doubts, but only because she'd never really cared for Homer all that much. She accepted him because he was part of Katie's life.

Or had been.

All right, so life didn't come with any guarantees. What was it Rex had called it? Trade-offs, but few real solutions. She could accept that. For eleven years she'd been married to a wonderful man, and she'd done everything in her power to be the sort of wife he'd needed. She'd lost her parents in an airplane crash, but she'd had her grandparents to hang on to until she could function again. She'd been widowed at thirty-one, and her grandparents had been gone by then. She'd needed them badly, but she'd survived. And bit by bit she'd managed to reconstruct her life.

Nor had she done a bad job of it. Although she might not be as outgoing and confident as Katie—who thought nothing of hopping a plane and flying out to the West Coast to wine and dine a prospective buyer for her clients' wares—she did all right. She did more than all right. She'd accomplished the major portion of Andrew's dream with no help from anyone. More important, she'd had sense enough not to punish herself because she couldn't do it all.

She'd offered a home to Andrew's elderly cousin, for obviously the poor woman had expected to be remembered in his will. Miss Beulah had declined, making Lu feel slightly guilty, though the woman had property of her own and was hardly in need. Still, Lu couldn't say she hadn't been relieved at not having to share her home with the old tartar. It was bad enough having a bronze-and-granite monument as a constant reminder of the responsibilities of being a Lavender. Living with a woman who recited genealogical charts at the drop of a hat would have driven her clean up the wall.

But she'd offered. She could pride herself that she'd done her duty to Andrew, to his only remaining relative, to Parrish Falls and to the whole county school system. And now, dammit, it was about time she did her duty to herself.

Last night had been a revelation to her. Either she'd forgotten a lot over the past few years, or there were a lot of things she'd never even learned.

Lu stretched slowly, closing her eyes with a smile of sheer delight. Parts of her that hadn't felt this way in ages now ached with a delicious tenderness. Rex had been a gentle lover, but no man of his size and temperament could help but leave his mark on a woman.

Lu had recognized the control he'd exerted; today she was grateful. At the time, she'd only been impatient.

It had been sheer instinct that had prevented her from inviting him to stay the night, not the thought of tomorrow, or of what the neighbors might say. She hadn't invited him upstairs to the bedroom she'd shared with Andrew because common sense had warned her to take things one step at a time.

Lu had loved Andrew with all the ardor of a young, inexperienced girl for her first lover. The fact that he had been older and much more sophisticated had sometimes been a plus, sometimes a minus. Theirs had been a good relationship, but she was a woman now, not an impressionable girl. A different woman from the one who had married Andrew, different even from the woman who had mourned him. Somehow, without her noticing when it had happened, she had grown and changed.

Now it was time to love again. Now there was Rex. Lying here in her bed in the clear light of day, she thought it all seemed so simple.

The clear light of day? Great Scott, what time was it?

"Nine-twenty-seven!" she screeched, leaping out of bed. Her alarm hadn't gone off. Worse still, she hadn't even remembered to set it!

Moments later, with the bath water running, she dialed her office and explained that her alarm clock hadn't gone off and that she was going to be at least an hour late. It didn't help to remember that she had a dental appointment at eleven, and the temp they'd hired last week was a charming dimwit. "So much for handling things in a capable, adult manner,'' she muttered as she pawed frantically through her closet for something that wouldn't melt before she got to work.

Rex brought his portable computer into the motel room and set it up. He'd had a backlog of messages at his office when he'd checked in with Chloe, who'd told him that if he didn't claim his mail soon, she and Max were going to have to rent a larger house. The first thing he had to do was wind up the Davis job with a final report. After that, he would return a few of the most pressing calls. There was a sheaf of messages from the Delaware plant, a couple more from the people up in Maine. He'd better get off his butt and do something about them or he'd lose both jobs. He wasn't the only consultant in the field, he reminded himself.

Meanwhile, what the hell was he going to do about Lu Lavender?

Three hours later he came up for air. The pot of coffee he'd ordered sent to his room was cold, and his head was splitting. He'd been afraid all along that the Davis plant would turn out to be one of those border-line operations where there was no real solution to the bulk of the problems.

Hell, they'd known the score. They hadn't needed a consultant to tell them they were in trouble. Most of the equipment had come over on the ark, and they were too far from the river to co-generate with hydro. The cost of the scrubbers required to keep the emissions legal on these old coal burners was prohibitive.

Even to begin to cover it, the rates would have to triple. The best he could do was lay out a plan of gradual replacement that would ease specific problems, but there was no way around the fact that they were going to have to go to a much higher grade of coal. Which meant higher costs. Which meant dealing with the utility board, the stockholders, and a bunch of customers who didn't want to hear about another rate increase.

Tiredly he pressed his thumbs against his eye sockets. Why had he deliberately chosen a field where the problems were apt to be unsolvable? An unconscious need to punish himself?

His mind threatened to stray again, and he shoved back his chair and stood up. He had to get out of here. He had to get the hell out and breathe some genuine air instead of this prepackaged stuff they supplied for cheap motels.

The trouble wasn't with the job, and he knew it. It was Lu. Even for a man who'd made some beauts, he was beginning to suspect that last night he'd made one of the major mistakes of his life.

There'd been a few times—not many, but a few—when he'd wondered if his whole life wasn't one big mistake. The woman who'd brought him squalling into the world some forty-one years ago had evidently thought so. She'd kept him around long enough to milk a few bucks out of his old man and then she'd farmed him out to whoever needed an extra pair of hands.

By the time the state of Texas had stepped in, the old man had walked off a ferryboat into eighteen feet of water and never come up again, and she'd moved on to greener pastures, leaving Rex with a small-time fish packer who didn't care who headed his shrimp as long as all ten fingers flew at maximum speed. Like the other kids who'd hung out on the waterfront, he'd been paid well below minimum wage, but he'd made out okay.

Big for his age, he'd hustled the wharfs, packing fish, heading shrimp, earning a buck here, two bits there. And he'd learned. He hadn't much liked working for the sportsmen, the fiberglass yachtsmen with their careless kindness and their equally careless cruelties, but he'd learned from them. He'd learned a hell of a lot. He'd preferred the commercial fishermen, the men who wrested a living from the water, making expenses one day, going in the hole the next, always hoping for the one big catch that would set them up. He'd learned from them, too.

From his own father he'd learned nothing. His mother had whined about the wonderful life she'd given up when she'd married the bum. Neither of them, to his knowledge, had ever done an honest day's work. Nor had they ever laughed.

The commercial fishermen had laughed. He'd liked that. He'd liked their independence, and the fact that while they might gripe about conditions, they kept coming back, kept going out. Kept on working and dreaming.

He'd learned how to laugh. As he grew up, he'd carried in the back of his mind the dream of working hard and earning the right to a home of his own. Kids, too. Oh, yeah, he'd wanted a kid—maybe two. But first he had to be certain he could look after them.

It was crazy; no one knew that better than he did. He hadn't the slightest idea where such a damned fool idea had come from, but what the hell, even the mangiest cur dreamed, didn't he?

Thanks to a foster mother who'd been even tougher than he was, he'd managed to scrape through high school. Afterward he'd landed a job with a small construction outfit and discovered that building was something he got a lot of satisfaction from. He'd been seeing Kelli Crawford for several months by then. She'd wanted to move in with him when he'd rented his first two-room apartment, but Rex had insisted on marriage.

With both of them working and going to school nights, it hadn't been an ideal situation. Still, he'd been on top of the world. A few more years, he'd figured, and they would be able to put a down payment on a house and maybe start a family.

He should've known it was too good to be true. The promotion, for instance. He'd never forget how proud he'd been when he'd been called into the boss's mobile office. "Now, we ain't one o' the big boys, son," Pug Conners had said. "Not yet, we ain't, but we're settin' pretty at a time when all the big boys is hog-tied in gov'ment red tape. Seein' how we're kinda small and informal, you might say, we can get in, get the job done, and get out while they're still busy fillin' out six miles o' gov'ment forms."

Red tape hadn't interested Rex at the time. He'd liked seeing things get built and being a part of it.

"I'll be honest with you, boy, we can't pay you what you're worth, not yet we can't, but if you want in on the ground floor, why by damn, you're in! I'll shake on it right here 'n' now! How's foreman sound to you?"

It had sounded great. So had all the other promises.

"We finish up this job before the first o' the month, and then I got a line on something big over on Pelican Island that's gonna put us in high cotton. You might as well forget about that fancy engineerin' degree you're so dead set on gettin', son. I got big plans for you."

The big plans had materialized five days later.

They'd been working three shifts, and as a new foreman, Rex had worked eighteen hours straight, gone back to the apartment and crashed for four hours, then returned to the building site. The first thing he'd seen was the pile of dry, pink earth as the back hoe angled around for another run. "Hey, where the hell's the bulkheading? Cab, you and Jerry get outta that trench! I ordered that stuff to be delivered first thing. You know better than—"

Without waiting to see that they obeyed his orders, he'd headed for the trailer that served as site headquarters for the small construction outfit.

"Where the hell's that bulkheading, Pug? Mac wasn't supposed to start trenchin' until we finished grading the other side! Now, dammit, we've got a bunch of unreinforced trenches and they're already in there startin' to lay pipe!"

"Now, son, don't go gettin' your gut in an uproar. I'll take care of any bulkheadin' I figger we need. You got any idee how much that stuff costs to rent?"

"I can't work a crew under those conditions."

"Calm down, boy. We'll be in and outta there before the dust settles. How long you think it takes to lay those lines?"

"Dammit, didn't you *hear me?* We can't afford the risk!"

"Hey, hey—lighten up!" The red-faced man had shifted his cigar. "You ain't been made chairman o' the board yet, boy. Now you get on out there and tell 'em to shake a leg an' leave the details to me. You want bulkheadin', you got it. I'll put through the call right now, but we ain't holding up to wait for it, y'hear? We get that pipe laid before the rain starts, or we don't—"

He'd felt it then, right through the soles of his thick, dusty boots. The sound had come a split second later. Not the sound of the cave-in, but the sound of men screaming. It was a god-awful sound, one he'd never forget as long as he lived.

Leaving Pug staring after him, he'd jumped out the door and landed running. The whole scene was enveloped in a cloud of pink dust, and he'd plunged in not even feeling it when he'd tripped over the back hoe.

He'd managed to pull both men out, but he'd had to dig for Jerry, and it had taken too long. Much later, someone said he'd been cursing all the time. He thought he'd been praying.

The papers had been served practically before the cast was dry on his foot. Numb with shock, he'd still thought he was just being subpoenaed as a witness. Not until later had he learned that Jerry's stepfather had filed suit against him for the boy's death.

Manslaughter. Wrongful death. Criminal neglect. He'd heard all those terms and more. Jerry had been nineteen. His friends and family had been both emotional and outspoken in their grief.

Rex had been totally out of his element when it came to protecting himself from the media, too numb even to know what he was saying. He'd felt guilty for not dragging both boys out before he'd gone to tackle Pug, and the guilt had come through clearly, both in the news reports and in the courtroom.

Pug had been unavailable. A seizure of some sort brought on by shock and mental anguish, his doctor had said. The physician had signed an affidavit declaring the head of the construction firm unfit to attend the hearings.

Rex had declared him unfit to walk the face of the earth, but by that time, no one had cared what Rex had thought. According to the evidence, Rex had been the one to call and cancel the bulkheading Pug had ordered delivered to the site. According to the testimony, the young foreman had been the one to send the deceased into an unreinforced trench after being warned repeatedly about taking chances. According to Pug's statement, Rex had been determined to prove himself by bringing in the job under cost.

Cab—Calbert Swain—had been a dead loss as a witness, claiming that because of shock, the whole incident had been wiped from his mind. He couldn't remember, according to his muttered responses.

Couldn't remember anything that had happened that day. Not until much later had Rex learned that Cab's invalid mother had accepted a large cash payment in exchange for her son's loss of memory.

The deck had been stacked so blatantly that anyone but an idiot would have recognized it. In spite of all odds, including a few juvenile skirmishes with the law, Rex had remained an optimist. It was all a big mistake, he'd kept telling himself. He'd kept waiting for the truth to come out, for someone who knew what had happened to step forward and clear him.

It hadn't happened. In disbelief, he'd watched the proceedings wind to an end, his inexperienced lawyer no match for the opposing one, a wily old Texan with half a century of experience. They hadn't stood a chance.

He'd seen Kelli only once during the drawn-out proceedings. She'd moved in with a friend and only went back home to pick up her things and to tell him she was filing for divorce.

By then, he'd hardly cared. Nothing had seemed very real to him. He'd been found guilty of causing the death of another man, the plaintiff had been awarded a staggering settlement, which he hadn't a hope in hell of collecting, since Pug's insurance company had reneged and Rex had nothing left but the clothes on his back.

Ironically it had been the same man who'd set him up who was eventually responsible for his being exonerated. Pug, seizure or no, had got out of Galveston almost before the dust had cleared, setting himself up in business north of Houston under a different name.

Less than a year later, he'd been under investigation for trying to bribe a member of the city planning commission. An enterprising reporter for the *Houston Chronicle* had remembered the Galveston incident and started digging. By the time he'd located Cab Swain, the boy's conscience had done a job on him, and the whole story had come out.

It had taken time, but Rex had been completely cleared. Only by that time, he'd had no wife, no home and no job. He hadn't had the guts to try for another job in construction. Not around Galveston.

Oh, sure—he'd been bitter. Who the hell wouldn't have been? But the habit of survival had been too deeply ingrained. He'd jumped the first freight headed east and never looked back.

God, that had been twenty years ago!

Leaning back in the uncomfortable chair, Rex stretched his long legs out as far as he could. He hadn't done too badly for himself, all things considered. In a fit of recklessness, he'd joined the army, and that had been the best thing that had ever happened to him.

Once he'd had the starch knocked out of him a few times, he'd settled down. It had given him a leg up on his engineering degree, which he'd finished later. He'd made a few friends along the way, as well, some that had lasted through the years. Max and Chloe, for instance. He and Max had gone through basic together and hit it off. They'd kept in touch, neither having any other family, and when Max had married Chloe, Rex had rented a tuxedo to serve as best man, split the

shoulder seams of the coat before the night was over
and ended up having to buy the damned thing.

It had been worth every penny. Max and Chloe were
more like family than anything he'd ever had.

Oh, he'd done all right for a wharf rat who'd seen
the inside of a cell more than once. He had himself a
couple of degrees, some healthy investments, a portable office and enough business to keep him occupied
sixty-five weeks a year.

The only problem was that he was starting to dream
again. And John Rex Jones had learned the hard way
that dreaming could be hazardous to your health.

It seemed to Lu that no sooner did she finish with
one deadline than another one rose up to haunt her.
This time it was the adjustments needed by an in-
creasing number of their clients in their September
quarterly estimated tax payment, to accommodate the
latest IRS ruling. With more clients calling for ap-
pointments every day, their business was growing
faster than Parrish Falls could supply help.

They'd hired a part-time temporary until they could
find someone more qualified. As for Gigi's qualifi-
cations, she had the world's sweetest disposition. Period. She could answer the telephone and take a simple
message as long as the caller spoke slowly, enunciated
clearly and spelled every other word.

On the best of days, Lu was limp by the time she left
the office. On a day when she'd overslept, when she
had to have a lost filling replaced, and when her mind
was somewhere in the stratosphere and refused to
come down to earth, she was a basket case.

If she'd hoped to hear from Rex during the day, she'd been disappointed. But then, he probably had his own deadlines. Neither of them was in a position to take time out to dwell on what had happened to them. Perhaps tonight. She'd cook him a special dinner, and afterward they would go upstairs to her sitting room and talk.

Yes, tonight...

It occurred to Lu as she backed out of her parking slot behind the small office complex and headed west on Hattie Street that if Rex had spent as much time staring into space with a silly grin on his face as she had today, they might as well both have stayed home from work.

He was probably waiting for her right now, she thought, chafing at the thirty-five-mile-an-hour speed limit. Parked under the poplar tree for the scant shade it provided, waiting for her to get home. She should have taken time to apply fresh makeup before she left the office. Her hair was a mess, too. Maybe she could distract him long enough to dash upstairs and run a brush through.

There was no one parked anywhere on her side of the street, no one waiting for her. Lu suppressed her disappointment. After all, Rex had a job to do, too. He'd probably left work about the same time she had and raced back out to the motel for a shower and a change.

After unlocking the door, she headed directly for the stairs, unbuttoning her dress as she went. If she hurried she could get a shower first.

On the other hand, the minute she got in the shower and turned on the water, he would be sure to call. Maybe if she took the receiver off, he would know she was home and call back. Or come around without even taking time to call.

Not until she'd showered and dressed, made herself a sandwich and then brushed her teeth and touched up her makeup again, did Lu begin to worry. Surely she should have heard from him by this time. Had he said anything last night to indicate that he would be out of touch for a while?

Curling up in the blue chair in the stuffy little downstairs parlor, which had suddenly become one of the her very favorite rooms in the house, she stared at the sofa across the room as if concentration alone would conjure up the man who had made love to her three times less than twenty-four hours ago.

Lying side by side, staring up at the marble-patterned paper on the high ceiling, they had talked. Lu had deliberately tried to lead him into telling her something about his childhood—something besides the apple-stealing episode. He'd told her that both his parents were dead, and that he'd lived with foster parents for several years. Not until much later had she realized that between that outrageous Texas act of his and the kisses he seemed determined to plant on every square inch of her body, she'd learned little that she hadn't already known. Which was little indeed.

Not that she needed to know any more to fall in love with him.

Not that she was ready to call it love, either, she reminded herself—at least not until she had some clearer indication from him that it wasn't entirely one-sided.

Of course it wasn't one-sided! Her heart knew the difference, even if her cautious mind would rather hear the actual words. There'd been something special between them right from the beginning, even though Rex had deliberately confused the issue.

They'd both been wary, but they'd both been attracted, too. And after last night, it was more than attraction, at least on her part.

Dammit, the *least* he could do was to call! Lu twisted restlessly, wincing as she felt a twinge in her lower back. It was no more than she deserved for necking on a rock-hard horsehair sofa and making out on the floor like a kid half her age.

Which didn't make her feel a bit better.

By eight forty-five she was hiccupping. Torn between anger and worry, she swore softly. Unlike last night the streets were clear now. The power crews had patched up enough lines last night to restore most of the town's power and come back today after she'd left for work to clear up all the downed limbs and the debris caused when a truck had skidded into the light pole on the corner.

She would give Rex until nine, and then she was going to turn out the lights, lock up the house and go to bed. Then she would probably lie awake until all hours calling herself every kind of fool for letting herself be taken in by some smooth-talking stranger.

Had it only been a diversion for him? She could have sworn it hadn't. No man could be that convincing with a woman who meant nothing to him...could he?

That was the trouble, she didn't know. She'd had absolutely no experience with this sort of thing, and all her old insecurities were rising up to haunt her. Tapping her foot, Lu told herself to be calm, that there had to be a perfectly logical explanation, that any minute now the phone would ring and it would be Rex to say he was on his way after changing three flat tires, and they'd laugh about all her doubts.

Any minute now.

Eight forty-eight. Eight forty-eight and a half! *"Damn!"*

Restlessly, she began prowling. Either the air conditioner was set too low or she was getting hot under the collar. The sound of her heels were muffled by the aged rugs as she strode into the foyer and checked the thermostat. It was set right where she always left it. Where the man from the museum told her she should leave it for maximum protection of the art collection.

The art collection. *Everything* was for the maximum protection of the art collection! What about *her* maximum protection? Didn't she count anymore?

Eight fifty-one. *Hiccup!* One of these days she was going to trash the whole damned Andrew C. Lavender Collection and get involved in something more her speed. Like a pig farm! Who needed a man, anyway? She would buy herself a farm! She would rather take care of a bunch of pink squealing porkers any day than an abomination like that Tennisson thing.

Turning toward the gallery, she glared at the offending canvas. Or rather at where it should have been, but wasn't.

Eight

Rex slammed down the phone with an oath born of frustration, impatience and worry. Of all the dumb ideas he'd ever had in his life, this one was right up there at the top of the list. It had all seemed so logical to him this morning when he'd finished up the Davis report, all things considered.

Such as the fact that if he hadn't forcibly restrained himself, he would have carried her out of that damned museum of hers last night and found a place—a cave in the mountains—anyplace where they could be alone together until he could talk her into marrying him.

Such as the fact that he'd been riding the thin edge for too many years, insisting on keeping his ties, even his business ones, to the minimum in case he had to move fast.

He'd moved fast, all right. Fast enough to have built up a decent-enough reputation as a power plant consultant so that it was about to work him to death. Fast enough so that outside Max and Chloe and a few other people scattered across the country that he'd pretty much lost track of, his life was totally arid.

No wonder he was such a dead loss when it came to handling a serious relationship. He'd steered clear of them for twenty years. He sure hadn't been looking for one when he'd taken on a job in a little valley town in the back of nowhere.

Fishing the coins out of the return slot, he tried again. He'd driven by her house as soon as he'd finished up out at the plant, to tell her he was going to make a quick run to Richmond, collect his mail and a few clothes, and he would be back sometime the next day.

Only she'd left for work, of course. He'd gone to her office, only to find out that she'd just left for an appointment. As he hadn't the least idea of what kind of appointment, where it was or how long it would take, he'd settled for leaving a message, knowing that the more he delayed leaving, the more his return would be delayed. He'd been chafing at the bit as it was, unwilling to be gone from her for more than a few hours at most.

He'd left the message, planning to call from the road, only her phone had rung busy every damned time he'd tried. He'd finally succeeded in getting someone to break in with an emergency message that he'd been called out of town unexpectedly, only to be told that the line was out of order.

He'd chugged half a pack of antacids, driven like a bat out of hell to the next town along the way and tried again, with the same results.

Somewhere along the way, Rex had been forced to admit that his reasons for running hadn't been all that clear-cut. There'd been an element of panic involved. Once he'd admitted it to himself and examined it, he'd been able to come to terms with it.

Sure he was scared. Hell, who wouldn't be? Every time he started building a life for himself—every time he thought he had it made—something happened, and he wound up flat on his back. And every time, it cut a little closer to the bone. There'd been a few times over the past twenty years when he'd looked at a woman and considered the possibility of settling down, but always before he could make up his mind, the doubts would begin to creep in, and he would move on again.

Some guys were meant to be loners, he would tell himself—usually late at night and with a few drinks under his belt. He'd had a long, successful run as a loner. Why tamper with fate?

And then he'd met Lu.

The first thing Lu did was look in the other two rooms. As if she could have accidentally mislaid something so large and grotesque, or forgotten which room she'd hung it in.

She would have to call someone if it was truly missing. The museum? Oh, Lord, how awful! This was the first time she'd ever taken advantage of their loan program for regional nonprofit galleries, and she'd only squeaked through the requirements by a hair.

Well, who, then—the police? That was silly. It certainly wasn't a theft. It *couldn't* be a theft. In the first place, she had a perfectly good burglar alarm, and in the second place, no one in his right mind would want the thing. Certainly no one in Parrish Falls. Except perhaps the postman who used to be a crop duster, but he lived in a mobile home and it probably wouldn't go through the door, even if his wife would allow it inside.

Clutching one elbow, her chin resting on her fist, Lu paced. Oh, this was ridiculous! Things like this didn't happen in Parrish Falls. *Nothing* ever happened in Parrish Falls.

In the end there was nothing to do but call the police. The thing was obviously missing. Something had happened to it, and she seriously doubted that it had been programmed to self-destruct after the first wave of criticism.

The good part was that it took her mind off a more pressing problem, she thought as she waited for the dial tone. And waited. And waited.

"Oh, darn," she muttered after jabbing repeatedly at the button. The thing had been working that morning when she'd called the office, but evidently in clearing away the debris from the storm, the crew from the power company or someone had yanked something loose.

She dashed out the front door with the intention of asking the neighbor across the street if she could borrow her phone. Unfortunately Lana Potts waylaid her before she even got out of her front yard.

"Is everything all right, Tallulah?"

Lu shook her head distractedly. This was no time for another lecture on the pitfalls that lay in wait for a woman living alone.

"I've seen a lot of mighty peculiar goings-on over there, and I was just wondering..."

"Everything's just fine, Mrs. Potts, except that the power crew must have done something to my phone when they cleaned up today. I was going to report it."

"Come on in and use mine. It's still working. I was just talking to Rebecca down at the water company, but when I saw you run outside I thought I'd better check on you."

I'll just bet you did, Lu thought. Reluctantly she followed the older woman into a house much like her own. She was tempted to report her phone out and let the call to the police station wait, but it might be days before she got service again. There was only one repairman.

The first call made, she asked if she could make another, and then waited a moment to see if Mrs. Potts would have the decency to give her a bit of privacy. She might have known better. Her hostess plopped down in a chair, raised her skirts half an inch above her knees and began fanning herself with the latest copy of *Good Housekeeping*.

"Bill? This is Lu Lavender. I wonder if you could drop by sometime this evening. Oh...tomorrow, then? No, it's nothing serious, I'll tell you all about it when I see you. No, I didn't lose any trees last night." She listened to a recital of who had suffered storm damage and which creeks were at flood stage, and why Bill, two county deputies and at least half the volunteer fire department had been out all night and most of the day.

With a sigh, she put down the phone, casting a glance at her hostess, who was taking in every word.

"Would that be Bill Peagram over to the station? I thought something was wrong over there." She nodded several times and struggled to her feet.

"Don't bother to see me out, Mrs. Potts. And thanks for the use of your phone." Lu had hoped for a clean escape, but just as she cleared the ligustrum hedge, she heard Lana Potts's screen door creak open and the sound of a porch rocker being dragged into viewing position.

She might have known she would be under surveillance by half the town the minute she put through a call to the police. Lana had probably managed to pass the word to Rebecca for general release before she'd come outside. Any minute now Mr. Cahill would stroll by, and Miss Kingsley on the corner would come out to walk her dog.

Lu supposed she ought to be thankful, but at the moment, all in the world she wanted was Rex's solid, reassuring presence, his arms to hold her, that deep, Texas drawl of his to tell her everything was going to be all right, that someone had just hidden the thing as a prank.

But who? More to the point, how? Her house had been locked up solid all day, with a foolproof burglar alarm that rang directly in the police station.

Of course, there were only three men on the force, and Bill had admitted that they'd been pretty tied up since the storm. The whole valley was flood prone af-

ter a hard rain, and last night's had been a gully
washer.

It was late. Between worrying about Rex and worrying about that damned painting, she probably
wouldn't get any sleep at all. She would have given
anything if she could have turned the whole puzzling
mess over to Bill Peagram tonight so that she could
concentrate on being miserable over Rex.

Could she have absentmindedly carted the thing up
to the attic? The idea had occurred to her the first time
she'd seen it. No, she would have remembered. She
wasn't *that* far gone. Besides, she would have had
problems with the lack of headroom on the attic stairs.

Who would profit from stealing it? It was insured,
of course, but any insurance money collected would go
to the museum. Or the artist? Why would an artist
steal his own painting? For publicity?

This was getting her nowhere. She might as well go
to bed and lie awake worrying about Rex. If she was
going to be miserable, at least she could spend her
emotions on something worthwhile.

"Yes'm. Lessee now—no strangers, burglar alarm
not working, phone not working, no sign of forced
entry except for where a piece of tape was stuck over
the plate on the side door. I b'lieve that about does it,
Miz Lavender. By the way, do you keep a list of visitors, like a guest book or some such thing? It might be
helpful to know who was here on Sunday."

Lu thought about the boys she'd caught smoking.
Surely they wouldn't...? No. They probably couldn't
even lift the thing off the wall. If they'd stolen any-

thing, it would probably be one of the watercolor nudes. "I don't keep a book, but I'll see if I can remember." A few minutes later she handed him a list. "I think that's all except for a couple from Florida who're staying at Banner Elk. They were driving a Mercedes convertible with one of those wrinkled dogs in the back. I don't think they'd have had room for the Tennisson, too."

"Not likely. Woulda taken something like a truck or a van. The way they make car doors these days..." He shook his head. "I'll be in touch, Miz Lavender. Meanwhile, you want to get that burglar system of yours fixed. Paid enough for it, if I remember correctly."

Lu let him out and avoided looking to see how many of her neighbors just happened to be sweeping their front walks. Maybe she'd better post a progress report on the front gate. Or a lack of progress.

At least her phone had been fixed. She'd called the Peacock first thing, asking for Rex Jones. His phone had gone unanswered, but he was obviously still registered there, or she would have been told otherwise. After the tenth ring on the fourth try, she gave up. There were only so many places in a small motel room a man could hide to avoid answering the phone.

She was late for work again, and this time she didn't even care. Sometime between midnight and daybreak, she'd reached a few conclusions about her life and the direction it was taking.

Or rather the lack of direction.

"I forgot to tell you, Mrs. Lavender, but a man came by yesterday," Gigi said as Lu sat down at her desk and reached for the stack of mail to be dealt with.

"Congratulations," she said sourly. Men were one of the reasons Gigi would never get far in this world.

"Oh, no, this one was yours," the young temp said earnestly. "He said to tell you, ah, something about— wait a minute, I wrote it down somewhere...."

Lu bit back a sharp remark. Gigi was no ball of fire, but she did her best. At least she wrote things down, even if they weren't always intelligible.

"Well...I can't seem to lay hands on it. Maybe I threw it out with yesterday's reminders." Lu groaned. "Anyway, I remember what he said. He was leaving. Is he a country-western singer, Mrs. Lavender? He sounded like he could be. For a man his age, he was sorta neat."

With great restraint, Lu refrained from strangling the girl. "Did he happen to say where he was going, Gigi? Or how long he'd be gone? Please try to remember. It could be important."

Carefully penciled eyebrows puckered over blue-frosted eyelids. "I don't think he said, but I did tell him you were at the doctor's."

Lu ground down on her new filling and said with careful emphasis, "The dentist."

"Yes, ma'am. I told him you had an appointment, but that you'd probably be back after a while."

"Probably! You knew damned well I'd be back! Why didn't you make him wait? Why didn't you find out— Oh, forget it."

Her shoulders drooped. There was no point in be-
laboring the point now. Gigi had done the best she
could, and either Rex would be back or he wouldn't.

Either way, Lu had a lot of arrangements to make,
and she might as well get started. Reaching for the
phone book, she looked up the number of the Lavender family lawyer.

Nine

Swamped by a load of work that had been piling up all week, Lu absently reached for the phone at five-fifteen on Tuesday afternoon, surprised to see that the day had fled, and with it Gigi, who shared the L-shaped office with her. She flexed her shoulders in an effort to relieve some of the tension.

"Richards and Scott," she answered automatically.

"Lu, could you please come down to the police station?"

She nearly dropped the phone. "Rex?" she managed to squeak, "Where on earth— What are you doing there? Where have you been? Are you all right? You haven't been in an accident, have you?"

There was none of the Texas drawl in evidence now. Instead he sounded . . . strange. "Please?"

"Three minutes," she promised, shuffling her stocking feet under the desk to locate her shoes. "I'll be there in three— Rex, are you *sure* you're all right?"

"Just hurry, will you?"

The speed limit didn't apply when your heart was in your throat, Lu told herself as she careened around the corner of Hattie and Westview in her dark blue Malibu. Had Rex learned something about the missing Tennisson? He might have seen something suspicious when he left the house Sunday night. They might even have the thief in custody. Maybe they'd even recovered the painting!

Oh, Lord, she hoped they'd recovered the painting! She'd never make fun of it again. As long as the museum didn't have to know she'd nearly lost the blasted thing, she would devote the rest of the month to singing its praises.

But the important thing was that Rex was back.

Parking on the corner by the fire hydrant in the only available space, she dashed halfway down the block to the small granite building and barged through the door. "Rex? Bill, where's Rex? Didn't he call from here?"

And then she saw him. Across the room, framed by the tall dusty window, his silhouette was unmistakable. "Oh, Rex, I was so afraid—"

"Can you identify this man, Miz Lavender?"

"*Identify* him!" Halfway across the floor, Lu swung around to stare at Bill Peagram in surprise. "Well, of course I can identify him."

"Lu, you don't have to get mixed up in this—" Rex began.

"Get mixed up in what? For goodness' sake, Rex, what's going on?"

His mouth clamped shut. His expression, his stance—everything about him—was forbidding. Even against the light, Lu could see that he looked ghastly. His color was gone and there was a stunned look in his eyes, as if he'd just walked away from a bad wreck. "I should never have called you, Lu. I'm sorry."

Something was wrong. Desperately wrong. It had nothing to do with any ridiculous painting, either. She looked from one man to the other, seeking a clue and finding none. Rex was obviously in some kind of trouble. He needed her—that had been a cry for help if she'd ever heard one—only now he was trying to pretend it wasn't.

"Rex, would you please tell me what's going on here? You called me—I came. Now the least you can do is tell me what we're both doing at the police station."

With a curt oath, Rex turned away to stare out the window at the setting sun. Lu was bewildered. She felt as if she'd woken up in the middle of a nightmare only to have the nightmare keep on unfolding around her.

"Can you positively identify this man, Miz Lavender?"

Exasperated, she swung around. "Well, of course I can identify this man! Didn't he tell you his name, for God's sake? Has he been in an accident?"

"Not so far's I know. He gave a name when we picked him up—John Jones—but when I tried to call the number on those phony business cards of his, I got the no-longer-in-service routine. I checked out the address, and it's a private residence, belongs to a couple that goes by the name of Beal.''

It had to be a nightmare. She'd been under a lot of stress lately, but nothing she shouldn't be able to handle. She was no stranger to stress. "Look, Bill, I don't know what's going on here, but if it's any help to you, then I positively identify that man as John Rex Jones, from Galveston—or Richmond.''

"Lu, you don't have to—''

"Hush up, Rex! If you won't talk, then one of us has to. I might not know what's going on here, but I do know you're in trouble, or else you wouldn't be here. And you *did* call me,'' she reminded him pointedly. Although she was beginning to wonder why.

Bill Peagram stood up, raked a hand through the few strands that covered his balding dome and ambled across to switch on the lights. A battery of harsh fluorescent tubes flooded the room with their unflattering light, and Lu's eyes went instinctively to Rex. She was unable to hold back a low cry of distress.

"Rex, are you sick? Have you been out there in that awful place all this time too sick to answer your phone?''

"What awful place is that, Miz Lavender?'' Bill asked, his patience growing frayed around the edges by too little sleep. He wasn't used to this much excitement. First the storm, then the robbery—a few more weeks like this and he was going to see about taking early retirement.

Ignoring him, Lu strode across to where Rex stood braced against the windowsill. He owed her some answers, and she was going to have them if she had to root them out the way her grandpop had tackled stubborn stumps—with dynamite. She'd had it up to *here* with this tall, silent macho stuff!

"Rex, I'm warning you," she began, but the warning was never completed. He looked awful! Everything about him, from the set of his shoulders to the bleakness of his eyes, cried, *Keep out! Private. No admittance.*

There was no way she could back off now, she was in too deep. Ignoring his signals, she planted herself before him, so close that she could feel the heat of his body, inhale the scent of his woodsy after-shave. "Is somebody around here going to tell me what's going on, or am I going to have to take this place apart, stick by stick?" she demanded, resisting the urge to gather him in her arms.

Shoving her roughly aside, Rex crossed the room and confronted the man behind the cluttered desk. "Look, officer, this lady doesn't know a damned thing. She's just somebody I happened to meet in the post office one day. I remembered her name, and I thought she might be able to identify me, that's all." The gasp he heard behind him twisted in his gut like a rusty knife. "Dammit, if you're booking me on suspicion of grand larceny, then why don't we get on with it? There's no point in keeping her around any longer, is there?"

Grand larceny? It took only a few seconds for things to click into place. There were still a few missing pieces, but Lu had heard enough. In two strides she was at Rex's side, all five feet five inches of her bristling with indignation. Grabbing a handful of rumpled khaki sleeve, she held him in place while she glared across the desk at the weary looking policeman.

"Bill Peagram, I don't know what you *think* you know about this man, but you don't know a darned thing, because he's lying through his teeth! Met him in the post office, indeed! His van was parked outside my house practically all weekend, and if you don't believe me, you can ask Lana Potts!"

Rex carefully disengaged her fist from his sleeve and stepped away from her, the look he turned on her somewhere between pity and scorn. Reeling from the impact, Lu could scarcely believe it when he said, "Stow it, Miz Lavender. You're a nice lady, and I'm sure you mean well, but I don't need any human sacrifices, thanks. Now why don't you just trot on back to that nice little picture gallery of yours and let me handle this? It doesn't concern you."

Lu felt hot color rush to her face, and then drain away, leaving her feeling weak and shaky. Pride urged her to walk out and leave him to his fate, but something that went far deeper than any pride refused to let her go.

Not until she was certain she could be calm and emotionless did she attempt a response. "Rex, I don't know what's going on, but I assume this all has something to do with the Tennisson painting." Nice lady, indeed! Her fine, sooty eyebrows lowered as she warmed to her topic. "As for you, you cornpone Casanova, you can get on back to Richmond or Texas or wherever any old time you want to go, but dammit, you're not taking the blame for something you

didn't do!'' Eyes blazing, she spun around and glared
at the policeman, whose mouth had fallen open. ''And
you, Bill Peagram, if you think this man is guilty
of . . . of stealing that repulsive painting, then you can
just think again, because Rex Jones never stole a thing
in his life, and I can personally vouch for that!''

Both men stared at her as if she'd suddenly started
breathing fire. Rex recovered first. ''Honey—Lu,
don't get mixed up in this. Please don't.''

''Miz Lavender, I don't know how well you know
this man, but I got a tip this morning about a suspicious-looking van seen hanging around your place
Sunday night, and it come back again Monday morning after you'd gone to work. Now, I ain't saying—''

''Good. I'd rather you wouldn't, because if you did,
I'm afraid I'd have to speak to my lawyer about—
about defamation of character and—and false arrest.
I think it's pretty obvious what the van was doing there
but if you'd like me to be more specific, I—''

''Lu, for God's sake,'' Rex agonized. His face had
gone from gray to red, and Lu felt a moment's doubt.
Was she taking too much on herself?

No, of course she wasn't. Whatever he was being
accused of, he didn't do it. She might not know where
he'd gone to school or what his mother's maiden name
was, or where he'd been for the past twenty-four
hours, but she knew the important things about him.
And the most important of all was that she loved him
more than she'd ever loved anyone or anything in her
life, whether he returned those feelings or not.

And dammit, nobody was going to get away with
accusing him of stealing an oversize, overpriced piece

of junk just because he happened to drive a van! "Of course he drives a van!" she yelled, when several moments passed during which both men just stared at her, neither of them uttering a word. "It's his office, for pity sake! And if you need another identifier, or whatever you call it—one he hasn't slept with—then call Edgar Hoag out at Davis Power Plant!"

Bill took out a handkerchief, mopped his perspiring face, carefully refolded the square and crammed it back in his pocket. "Ma'am, I'm just trying to get to the bottom o' this business."

Rex looked down at her as if she'd just popped out of a flying saucer. "Officer, I assure you that Mrs. Lavender is only doing what she sees as her civic duty. I'll admit I've been visiting the gallery to pick out a picture to give a friend as a graduation present, and yesterday—"

"In a pig's eye," Lu said succinctly. "You used that as an excuse to get in the first time, and you've practically camped on my doorstep ever since."

"Miz Lavender, this painting that got itself stolen is state property, you say? Reckon I'd better put in a call to Raleigh." He began opening and shutting desk drawers in halfhearted search for something or other.

Lu ignored him. Confronting Rex, her hand on her hips and her chin thrusting belligerently, she said, "You were there before daybreak Sunday morning, you were back right after lunch, and the Tennisson was certainly hanging there in plain sight when you left at a quarter of four on Sunday afternoon. You came back for supper and spent the night on my parlor floor—with me!—and don't you try to deny it, John

Rex Jones." She turned to the policeman. "Bill, I swear to you, if he'd tried to pry that thing off the wall with me sleeping not ten feet away, I'd have known it. Frankly I don't think he'd have had the strength even to lift it, not after—"

"Tallulah!" Rex roared.

"Lu . . . uh, Miz Lavender, you don't have to—"

"I don't care, this idiocy has gone far enough. I won't stand by and let you accuse this man of a crime when I happen to know that the only thing he ever stole in his life was a green apple, and—and he paid the price for that!"

Rex's arm went around her shoulder, and his other hand came up and closed gently over her mouth. "Officer, don't listen to her. I didn't steal the damned painting, that's God's honest truth, but as for the rest of what she said, Miz Lavender was just trying to protect me. I didn't spend the night in her bed. I'm sure you know her far better than to believe she'd— *Ouch!* For crying out loud, Lu, why'd you have to bite me?"

Ten

The ceiling fan spun lazily as Lu turned back the sheets. Rex was sprawled in her largest chair, a drink in his hand, the boots he'd just shucked covering a large portion of her dainty little hooked rug. She'd brought him directly up to her sitting room, gone downstairs and fixed them both a plate of sandwiches and a pot of coffee. The drink had been an afterthought. He'd needed it.

"Lu, why'd you do it? All you needed to do was tell Peagram I was who I said I was. I had enough documentation on me, but when my business address didn't check out, he got suspicious. I tried to explain about my arrangement with Max and Chloe Beal, and that I'd just this morning had my business phone taken out and changed my mailing address to a post office box number because they were having trouble with the zoning board, but he didn't buy it.''

''Why did you try to make it sound as if we hardly even knew each other? Were you afraid I'd try to take advantage of you? You know, that old Chinese thing about someone saving a life and having that life belong to them?''

''You know better than that.'' He drained his glass and sighed, his eyes half closed. He'd had practically no sleep in the past thirty-six hours, and it was beginning to tell on him. ''Besides, I don't think identifying someone for the cops has the same clout as saving their life. Lu, what are you doing?''

''Undressing. Why?''

Rex's red-rimmed eyes snapped open again and he stared at her. ''What do you mean, why? I mean . . . *why?*''

''I just felt like getting out of the things I wore all day at the office and into something more comfortable while you try to explain why you said all those rotten things to me in front of Bill Peagram.''

He groaned. ''Lu, I'm sorry about that. You have to understand, I was just trying to protect you. I mean, here you are, living in a hotbed of Lana Pottses, and some bum comes through town and—''

''And?'' she prompted. ''And what? Ruins my reputation? Has his wicked way with me? Debauches me? Or is that despoils—I never did know the difference, but they both sound sort of interesting.''

Rex levered his road-weary bones up from the comfortable depths of the chair, his rumpled khakis, discarded boots and rugged features looking excitingly masculine amid all the ivory wicker and pastel prints. He placed his hands on her shoulders, making no attempt to draw her to him. "And some bum comes through town, takes one look at you and falls so damned hard that he doesn't know what hit him. He makes a real jackass of himself trying to cover his feelings. The harder he falls, the more scared he gets and the worse he behaves. Lu, you have to understand, nothing like this has ever happened to me before—at least not in more than twenty years, and never to this degree. God, I still can't believe it!"

Lu had forgotten to breathe. Now she dragged in a deep, ragged gasp of air and lifted her hands to his chest. "Why couldn't you have told me?"

Rex shook his head. "You don't know a thing about me, Lu. A woman like you—you have no conception of what it's like growing up the way I did, running tough as a kid, in and out of trouble, finally landing on the right track only to get mixed up in something so ugly that it ruined my marriage and my career before I was old enough to know what the hell was going on."

"Then tell me, darling. Make me understand. Trust me that much, at least."

Trust her. It sounded so simple, but he'd learned the hard way that a man was a fool to trust anyone. Love only made you vulnerable. To give your trust was to hand someone the tools to destroy you.

Yet hadn't she trusted him? More than anyone in his life had ever trusted him, and with far less reason, knowing nothing about him, hadn't she taken his innocence on blind faith and defended him against one of her own?

Rex shook his head wonderingly. He still couldn't believe it—that someone so fine should care so much for a roughneck like him. If it took the rest of his life, he'd prove to her that her trust was not unfounded.

There in the quiet room that smelled of her light fragrance, surrounded with all the delicate and lovely artifacts of her sheltered life, Rex laid bare his past, leaving out nothing.

"So maybe now you can understand why I went a little haywire when I pulled up in front of this place about a quarter of five and stepped out of the van and into the custody of that overgrown bloodhound. All I could think of was that it was happening all over again. I sort of went crazy for a little while, I guess."

They were lying on their sides facing each other on the bed now, still fully clothed, although several of the buttons on Rex's shirt had come undone as Lu toyed with them. "Peagram's eyes popped out when he looked inside the van. I'd loaded it up with boxes and crates—cleared everything out of Max's place and dumped it in anything I could lay hands on, clothes and files all mixed up together. I don't know who was in a bigger hurry, me or Chloe. She's seven months along, and wanting to get the room done up as a nursery before she gets too big to do any papering and painting."

Lu slipped her hand inside the open shirt and began to tease the curls that patterned his chest. "So you called me to come identify you, and the minute I did, you tried to pretend you hardly knew me. Fine friend you turned out to be."

"I think it's called chickening out." He tucked a dark curl behind her ear and then lingered to trace the pink whorls with a fingertip. "All I know is the minute you walked through that door I knew I didn't want you mixed up in it anywhere, under any circumstances."

"Too late, love—I was mixed up in it the first time you ever tried to pick me up out on Power Plant Road. I've been getting in deeper ever since, and now I'm afraid I'm in so deep I'll never get out again."

Rex grinned. "Damned right you won't. You should have run when you had the chance, sweetheart, because I'm going to tie you up so tight you won't get loose in a hundred years."

"That ought to about cover it," Lu mused. Having traced the line of dark hair to his belt, she went to work on the buckle. "Poor Bill, he probably thought he'd solved every burglary in the past five years when he hauled you in. Pity I couldn't let him keep you, but I need you more than he does."

Rex covered her hand with his own, having discovered that he wasn't as tired as he'd thought. "Honey, you're playing with fire," he said grittily.

"I certainly hope so. You promised me a hundred years, but so far, all I've seen is one night."

"You nice ladies can be pretty demanding, can't you?"

"I'm a woman, Rex. When it comes to love, there's no such thing as a lady."

"I won't argue semantics with you. Whatever you are, you're what I want more than I've ever wanted anything in my life. Except maybe a hot shower and about ten hours' sleep."

"I believe that can be arranged," Lu said. "I'm sorry, Rex, you're totally exhausted and all I can think about is seducing you." She sat up and slid her feet to the floor, only to be hauled back onto the bed. Rex, his jaw bristling with late-day beard, glowered at her.

"How big is this shower of yours? I hope it's not one of those dinky little jobs, because what I have in mind takes a little room."

"Ooohh?" Lu drawled. It occurred to her that he didn't look nearly as tired as he had a moment before. "Would this have anything to do with debauching or despoiling?"

"Both?" He groaned. "Okay, I'll see what I can come up with along those lines. We mechanical engineers are noted for accomplishing the impossible against great odds."

He was a gifted engineer, Lu had to admit a short while later, as he heaped suds on her breasts and proceeded to wash them in the most ingenious way. Slowly he massaged lather down her back and over her hips. He knelt before her in order to continue his incendiary strokes, until she was clutching the chrome bar for support. "Oh, for goodness' sake, Rex, you don't have to—Rex, you *can't*!"

But he could. And did. Eyes shut tightly, Lu stiffened her legs, braced the back of her head against the shower wall and whimpered as skyrockets began shooting off in all directions.

Then he held her until she could stand unsupported again. Then she began covering him with handfuls of lather, stroking it over his chest and down over his flat stomach. "Honey, I'm warning you," Rex began, his voice strained almost beyond recognition.

"What long legs you have, darling," Lu purred, kneeling to slap a handful of bubbles on a shapely kneecap."

"Lu, for the love of—"

"My thoughts exactly," she whispered, stroking higher and higher until he was trembling with urgency. Nibbling gently, she savored the taste of him until he dragged her almost roughly to her feet. "Are you wanting to finish me off before I can even take out a marriage license? God, woman, I'm only human!"

He took her mouth in a hungry kiss that tasted of water and whiskey. Lu stood on tiptoe to wind her arms around his neck, pressing against his thrusting power until he lifted her up, fitting her legs about his waist. "I don't think this is too safe," he gasped, and it was the last rational thought either of them had until the world exploded and all the pieces began drifting through space.

Eventually, leaving a trail of wet footprints and damp towels behind, they collapsed on the bed. "Sorry about the short fuse, honey. Maybe when I'm not so tired . . ." Rex said sleepily.

Lu, sprawled halfway across him, managed a drowsy laugh. "Whose short fuse, yours or mine?"

"Hmm, come to think of it, you—"

"Shh." She lifted her head from his chest. "Rex, did you hear something?"

"Yeah. My voice. I was talking, remember?"

"No, silly, I mean something downstairs. Didn't you hear it?"

"Nope."

"Somebody ought to check it out."

"Somebody?" Rex said plaintively. "Where do you get this 'somebody' stuff? Whose house is this, anyway?"

"As soon as I can legally arrange it, it will belong to the city of Parrish Falls. Until then, it's mine, and what's mine is yours, cowboy, so how about putting on your pants and checking it out?"

"What do you mean, it'll belong to the town of Parrish Falls? What the devil have you done?" Rex sat up and stared down at her, his wet hair sticking every which way.

"Did you want to live here? I guess I can undo what I started, but I'd better warn you, it gets to be a pain having strangers tramp in and out of your house and having to keep up with all the paperwork of running a nonprofit gallery, and complying with all the—"

"Dammit, I don't care if we live in a packing crate, that's not the point! What made you decide to sell your home? You didn't mention anything about it before I left."

Lu shrugged. She was sitting up too by now, bare from the waist up. Her hair, as usual, was curling like the wool of a shaggy black sheep as it dried around her face. "Actually I'm giving it, not selling it. I've never felt as if it belonged to me, anyway. As for why, maybe I just suddenly realized that if I didn't like the way my life was going, then it was up to me to do something about it. So I did. I'm turning over the house to the city fathers, with Miss Beulah Lavender overseeing the historic part of it and Hector Perryman taking over the gallery. Hector's a pain but he's a dedicated pain.''

"And where did you propose to live?" Rex asked.

Lu looked at him uncertainly. "Um, maybe in the back of your van? Or if you hadn't come back, I thought I might see about finding something in the country."

Rex looked at her as if she'd lost her senses. "The country! Honey, I don't know how to break this to you, but Parrish Falls isn't exactly the hub of the universe."

"Oh, I know that, but it's got sidewalks and street-lights, and the houses are too close together. I just want a place where I can have a big garden and maybe a few chickens if I want to. Nothing fancy."

"How about a few acres of pasture land with maybe a pond and some nice whatchamacallit trees? Maybe something out on Power Plant Road?" He tried and failed to look nonchalant.

"Rex, we couldn't! Could we...?"

"We could sure as hell give it a shot, honey. My job's about as portable as they come. We could get a chicken sitter now and then and you could go with me..."

"Gus really doesn't use the land around the pond. I could go on working for Mr. Scott, and—"

"Shh! Did you hear something?" This time it was Rex who interrupted her to listen. "Stay here. I'd better check it out."

"Not without me, you're not," Lu said, scrambling out of bed even as Rex yanked his pants up around his hips. "Now that I've finally got you out of Bill Peagram's clutches, I'm not about to let anything else happen to you."

"Okay, but stay out of sight until I see what's going on, will you? I'm too tired to play hero tonight."

From the first floor came the sound of a thump, followed by a grunt and another thump. Rex was down the stairs like a shot, with Lu hurrying after him, buttoning her housecoat as she went.

"What the hell are you trying to do?" she heard him yell as he disappeared into the gallery. She waited to hear the response. He'd evidently caught someone red-handed.

"My hernia," whined a familiar voice. "Help me lift it, will you?"

"Hector?" Lu cried, hurrying down the stairs to confront the embarrassed-looking culprit, his white suit now liberally smeared with mud. "Hector, how *could* you!"

"I'm sorry, Tallulah, I hoped I could get it back inside without disturbing you." His skin looked yellow, and he was sweating heavily. One hand was pressed to his side.

"Oh, for goodness' sake, Hector, you're old enough to know you can't just walk in and cart off anything you don't happen to like. This is a public collection."

"I know, I know," the old man said remorsefully. He looked as if he were going to burst into tears. "I never actually stole it, you know. That is, I never got it any farther than the shed behind your garage. I just wanted to make people take me seriously for a change. Ever since Andrew came back from New York, people have lost all respect for my judgment.''

Lu moved past Rex and put an arm around the thin old shoulders. ''That's not true, Hector. But even if it were, you just can't go around inflicting your personal prejudices on everyone else.''

''Andrew did.''

''No, he didn't. Andrew hated some of the stuff here, but he considered them the best examples of a particular school of painting, and that's all that mattered. He never wanted to be an arbiter of taste any more than you do,'' she said diplomatically.

''Well...I suppose that's true enough. We in positions of public trust have to think of the larger truth.''

Later, after Rex had ushered the old man out, hung the painting and checked the doors, he followed Lu into the kitchen. ''We in positions of public trust?'' he repeated with a wry grin.

''He's something, isn't he? Rex, I don't want Bill Peagram to know what happened. As far as anyone else is concerned, some prankster hid the wretched thing for a joke.''

''Far be it from me to throw a wrench in the works. The sooner you unload this white elephant, the sooner we can take off on our honeymoon. That is, if you have no objections to a working honeymoon. I've got a couple of jobs under consideration, one in Delaware and one in Maine. Of course, if you'd rather wait until I get back...''

''Wait? You're not serious, I hope. Because if you think I'm letting you leave town without me, you're in for something of a shock." Lu ladled coffee into the filter, counting under her breath.

Rex wrapped an arm around her, nuzzling the top of her head with his chin. "Better make it extra strong, honey. Something tells me I'm not going to get a whole lot of sleep anytime soon."

"Another engineering project?"

Turning her in his arms, he brushed the wild curls from her face and gazed into her warm gray eyes. "Yeah," he said gruffly. "A long-term project, one that's going to keep us both busy for the foreseeable future."

"When do we get started?" Lu asked, her heart in her eyes.

"We already have, love. We already have."

*   *   *   *   *

MORE THAN A MIRACLE
by Kathleen Eagle

This month, let award-winning author Kathleen Eagle sweep you away with a story that proves the truth of the old adage, "Love conquers all."

Elizabeth Donnelly loved her son so deeply that she was willing to sneak back to De Colores, an island paradise to the eye, but a horror to the soul. There, with the help of Sloan McQuade, she would find the child who had been stolen from her and carry him to safety. She would also find something else, something she never would have expected, because the man who could work miracles had one more up his sleeve: love.

Enjoy Elizabeth and Sloan's story this month in *More Than A Miracle*, Intimate Moments #242. And if you like this book, you might also enjoy *Candles in the Night* (Special Edition #437), the first of Kathleen Eagle's De Colores books.

IM 242-1R

Silhouette Desire

COMING NEXT MONTH

AVAILABLE NOW:

TALES OF THE RISING MOON
A Desire trilogy by Joyce Thies

MOON OF THE RAVEN—June
Conlan Fox was part American Indian and as tough
as the Montana land he rode, but it took fragile yet
strong-willed Kerry Armstrong to make his dreams
come true.

REACH FOR THE MOON—August
It would take a heart of stone for Steven Armstrong
to evict the woman and children living on his land.
But when Steven met Samantha, eviction was the
last thing on his mind!

GYPSY MOON—October
Robert Armstrong met Serena when he returned to
his ancestral estate in Connecticut. Their fiery
temperaments clashed from the start, but despite
himself, Rob was falling under the Gypsy's spell.

Don't miss any of Joyce Thies's enchanting
TALES OF THE RISING MOON,
coming to you from Silhouette Desire.

SD 432